STRANGE BEDFELLOWS

Tess laughed.

"I know exactly what you're thinking, Mr. Know-it-all! You think I got elected to my office by sleeping with all the members of the Wyoming Stock Growers Association, don't you?"

"Well, not all of 'em," Longarm answered gallantly.

She asked in a worried childish tone if this meant he didn't want to help her win the November election after all.

Longarm said, "I still feel honor-bound to investigate a possible election fraud or not, Miss Tell . . . I promised I would before I ever knew you, in the Biblical sense or any other. Like I was saying before, there's business and there's pleasure. I try to keep 'em separate in my skull. If this Big Dick Wilcox is up to anything dirty, I mean to put a stop to it. If he ain't, I can't, whether the two of us act dirty or not. So . . . do you want to get dirty?"

DON'T MISS THESE
ALL-ACTION WESTERN SERIES
FROM THE BERKLEY PUBLISHING GROUP

THE GUNSMITH by J. R. Roberts
Clint Adams was a legend among lawmen, outlaws, and ladies.
They called him . . . the Gunsmith.

LONGARM by Tabor Evans
The popular long-running series about Deputy U.S. Marshal
Long—his life, his loves, his fight for justice.

SLOCUM by Jake Logan
Today's longest-running action Western. John Slocum rides
a deadly trail of hot blood and cold steel.

BUSHWHACKERS by B. J. Lanagan
An action-packed series by the creators of Longarm! The
rousing adventures of the most brutal gang of cutthroats ever
assembled—Quantrill's Raiders.

DIAMONDBACK by Guy Brewer
Dex Yancey is Diamondback, a Southern gentleman turned
con man when his brother cheats him out of the family for-
tune. Ladies love him. Gamblers hate him. But nobody pulls
one over on Dex. . . .

WILDGUN by Jack Hanson
The blazing adventures of mountain man Will Barlow—from
the creators of Longarm!

TEXAS TRACKER by Tom Calhoun
Meet J.T. Law: the most relentless—and dangerous—
manhunter in all Texas. Where sheriffs and posses fail, he's
the best man to bring in the most vicious outlaws—for a
price.

TABOR EVANS

LONGARM

AND
TOWN-TAMING TESS

JOVE BOOKS, NEW YORK

1419617

LONGARM AND TOWN-TAMING TESS

A Jove Book / published by arrangement with
the author

PRINTING HISTORY
Jove edition / August 2003

ISBN: 0-515-13585-2

A JOVE BOOK®
Jove Books are published by The Berkley Publishing Group,
a division of Penguin Group (USA) Inc.,
375 Hudson Street, New York, New York 10014.
JOVE and the "J" design
are trademarks belonging to Penguin Group (USA) Inc.

PRINTED IN THE UNITED STATES OF AMERICA

10 9 8 7 6 5 4 3 2 1

Chapter 1

Beavergame Banks said he'd cased the brick business-building across the way before dawn, slick as a polecat casing a henhouse before he circled in. But Swansdown Doris said she sensed a trap, adding, "They say Longarm is slicker than most marks, that he carries double-action cross-draw and moves like spit on a hot stovetop. And all that *before* one considers he's *the law*!"

The small dapper con man skulking in the dark doorway of a vacant store across from the dawn-lit offices of Portia Parkhurst, Attorney at Law, told the usually more fashionably dressed bottle blonde of, say, thirty, give or take a few hard times, "I told you the day I read about that famous Blackfoot jockey busting his neck in the Omaha Steeplechase that for all his rep, the one and original Longarm is more crippled up inside than many a mark we've taken to the cleaners full of Cupid's arrows, doll."

Sweeping his cunning eyes up and down the still-deserted downtown business street, Beavergame Banks confided, "I ain't carrying shit under this summer-weight frock coat, and I have it on good authority Longarm has a tough time hitting smaller men or drawing on an un-armed man. It's true he has been known to flatten smaller

1

men who've struck first, open-handed, firm, but fair. When *women* piss the big moose off, he just walks away from them, even when they're throwing things. Don't matter how big or tough a mark may *look* if he don't have what it takes to beat up smaller men or women!"

Swansdown Doris demurred, "He's *the law*! He don't have to beat up smaller men or women. He gets to *arrest* 'em, and you agreed to meet for the payment in his *lawyer's* office?"

Beavergame Banks said soothingly, "That's why I asked you to come along as my own legal counsel and witness. Longarm ain't about to arrest me or call my bluff. I told you he was crippled up inside. But even should he prove *willing* to drag the name of one of the only women he's ever loved through the muck and mire of a scandalous trial, I'm too slick to give him grounds for any arrest that'll *stick*. Like I told you back at our hotel when you dug in your pretty heels, it would be their word against our own. Blackmail's almost impossible to prove when one side *has* the other outwitnessed, and no district attorney of a town the size of Denver wants to clutter up his docket with a jury trial for a can of worms!"

"Somebody's coming!" Swansdown Doris hissed, crawfishing deeper into the storefront shadows.

"It's about time," growled Beavergame Banks. Then he cursed as he saw a couple of gents in business suits climb down from the hired hack to enter the offices across the way.

Swansdown Doris said, "All right then. Suppose he just tells you to go jump in the South Platte, or it turns out he don't have the money. How much does a deputy U.S. marshal draw in a durned year to begin with?"

As the hack pulled away, another suited figure came down the sunny side of the street on foot. But he wasn't Longarm either, damn it.

Resisting the yearning to light up, Beavergame Banks

2

told Swansdown Doris, "To answer dumb questions in order, should the mark refuse in front of his lawyer to pay up, we just smile, say he'll read all about it in the papers, and vamoose. We're less than a furlong from the Union Station, with trains lighting out in all directions and any direction being out of town."

He shrugged fatalistically and observed, "It happens that way sometimes. You got to know when to hold 'em. You got to know when to fold 'em, and you're no worse off when a fish gets off the hook than you were when you dropped your baited hook in the water."

He smiled, not in a nice way, and added, "They say he cried real tears when land-grabbers killed his Roping Sally from Switchback up in Montana Territory. They say he's done right by the Blackfoot kids who weed the flowers he planted on her grave as well. Like I said, a lovesick simp!"

In a small, lost voice, Swansdown Doris murmured something about the grave site she'd likely occupy all too soon.

Beavergame Banks continued. "As to Longarm having the wherewithal to buy discretion from a wandering newspaper stringer such as I, they don't pay higher-ranking lawmen enough to be worth our time. But our mark was fortunate enough to be sitting in with Poker Alice Ivers up in Leadville around the turn of the month, and it turned out to be his lucky night indeed!"

The pedestrian in the checked business suit turned in at the same entrance across the way as Swansdown Doris marveled, "Longarm *won* at cards with the notorious Poker Alice of the gold fields?"

Her parner in crime chortled, "It's strongly suspected Poker Alice *asked* Longarm to sit in, and it seems to be true the Limey gambling gal deals with considerable sleight of hand. For Longarm came out a real winner after he politely but firmly suggested Lurching Luke Longacre could be endangering his own health if he insisted on horning in on Miss Poker Alice's private game uninvited."

Swansdown Doris wrinkled her drinker's nose and said, "They say Lurching Luke never backs down and bad things happen if he fails to get his way. And we're going over yonder to *shake down* hardcase killers such as Lurching Luke are *afraid* of?"

"We surely are, if that hansom slowing down across the way means to stop where . . . Hot damn, it *has*! And if that ain't the one and original Longarm helping that woman in black down from their ride, he just sprung a twin brother! That gal he's with must be the female lawyer he was bragging about. We'll let them get on up to her office before we cross over. I already know which one it is. Her name's Parkhurst."

As their hansom drove off and the rather handsome couple entered the building across the way, Swansdown, Doris said, "I've heard tell of Portia Parkhurst too, she being one of the few single women out our way who ain't waiting tables or fucking for a living. They say she's sharp as a tack. I reckon a woman would have to be to take male lawyers on in court and beat 'em more than half the time! No shit, Beav, I think we ought to pass on this sting!"

Then the small, wiry, and surprisingly strong Beavergame Banks was half-steering and half-hauling her along as he growled, "You were never invited to think doodly-shit, Swansdown Doris. I recruited you as bait for my beaver games, somebody to fuck when I wasn't catching her in bed with marks, and on such rare occasions as this one to back my play as a witness to my purity!"

He hauled her up the stairs, and barely gave her time to smooth her features as he knocked imperiously on the office door lettered in gilt to read PORTIA PARKHURST, ATTORNEY AT LAW.

Longarm himself, standing over a foot taller than either

of them, was the one who opened the door and welcomed them to enter in a sullen tone. Seated at her desk with a window behind her framing her fine-boned head and the silver-streaked black hair pinned atop it, the severely handsome Lawyer Parkhurst was trying to seem older than her late thirties, and not getting away with it.

Swansdown Doris wanted to kill her. It just wasn't fair for another woman to be so trim in such a severe black poplin business suit.

Portia waved the two crooks to bentwood chairs Longarm had set up to face her desk. But even as they sat, she said, "You may as well know I have advised my client here to call your bluff. So for openers, just what have you got to sell?"

Beavergame Banks half-rose to hand her a few pages of carbon copy on onionskin paper as he confided in a reasonable tone, "Discretion. As a newspaper stringer or freelance reporter, I naturally took notes as the late Tim Medicine Dog lay dying in Omaha General after hitting a jump wrong and catching a whole lot of racehorse with his lower spine."

Portia glanced up at Longarm and murmured, "Custis?"

Her client shrugged and allowed, "Name rings a bell. Can't grow a face to go with it. Miss Sally's spread was barely outside the Blackfoot Reserve. She sold some of her beef to the B.I.A. So she often had Indian kids hanging about."

Beavergame Banks had risen from his seat to mosey over to a nearby doorway leading into another room of the office suite. Portia quietly said, "Mr. Banks, you said your name was?"

The con man threw the door open to step halfway into the other room. He turned back with a shrug, saying, "Just making certain it's a private conversation, ma'am. I'd best have a look inside that corner wardrobe now, if it's all the same with you-all."

Portia and Longarm exchanged weary looks. Before she could suggest he be her guest, Beavergame Banks had flung open the doors of the wardrobe standing in a far corner. In high summer, there was little to be seen in the way of clothing hung inside. Portia dryly asked if he cared to search her filing cabinets for whatever was eating him.

Sitting back down, the wiry con man said, "Just making certain it's your word against our own, Even Steven. As he lay dying, the Blackfoot, better known in racing circles, it appears, than back on the reservation, was asked by another reporter whether he had any wife or sweetheart back home to mourn for his life. That was when Tim Medicine Dog confessed on his deathbed to having loved and lost a forbidden white woman, the famous Roping Sally, to this even more famous Deputy U.S. Marshal Custis Long, or Longarm, as I'm sure most of our readers have heard tell of him."

Settling back in his seat and grinning, Beavergame Banks really seemed to enjoy adding, "Medicine Dog said he'd been wrangling a spell by day, and sweating harder at night for Miss Roping Sally, when Longarm here rode in like he owned Montana Territory and everybody in it to get her redskin lover fired and take his place in the, ah, depths of her fair white body."

Portia toyed with a pencil, but didn't write anything down as she murmured, "Just Roping Sally? No last names to go with such a fair white body?"

Beavergame shrugged and said he hadn't asked a dying Indian the last name of his forbidden love.

When Portia arched a brow at Longarm, he naturally could have told her the last name, but he chose to say, "They said she was an orphan gal, operating her old man's spread after he went under. I disremember their family name, if I ever heard it. Like I told you earlier, I never took Roping Sally away from nobody up Montana way that time. She sold beef to the Blackfoot Agency. I was

6

up yonder after killers who were working for a land-grabber out to cheat the Blackfoot. Seems I barely got to know poor Roping Sally before they killed her too. If any Indian, dead or alive, said he'd made love to Roping Sally before I showed up, he's a liar, dead or alive!"

Portia asked, "Then why are we holding this meeting with these shakedown artists, Custis? As Mr. Banks here explained about witnesses, we have your word against that of a dead Indian, for heaven's sake!"

Lounging on one arm of the leather chesterfield across from her desk, Longarm grumbled, "I don't want nobody gossiping about poor old Roping Sally, with her not here to defend her rep. Like I told this here smut peddler, I'm willing to pay *once* to keep such smut out of the papers. But I wanted a lawyer to tell me how to make sure these . . . never-minds don't come back the next time I'm in the chips to sell me the same fool smut!"

Portia shrugged and said, "You can't. That's why I advised you not to give them a plug nickel. But seeing you're so insistent on parting with your poker winnings, I've drawn up this *publisher's contract* for the both of you to sign."

When both men stared thunderstruck at her, the prim lawyer gal explained, "In exchange for the thousand dollars Mr. Banks demands for his silence, he'll be selling you all rights to publishing the last words he took down as Tim Medicine Dog lay dying."

Longarm allowed he didn't follow her drift. Beaver-game Banks grinned and said, "Sounds sensible to me. But I have to read anything twice before I John it with my Hancock!"

Portia handed three sheets of legal bond paper across the desk to the sly-faced Banks, saying they were duplicates to be signed in triplicate.

Swansdown Doris said, "Don't you do it! Can't you see she's trying to get you to sign a *confession*?"

"Confession to what?" snorted Beavergame Banks as he perused Portia's single-spaced contract. The con man chortled, "I could use a lawyer like Miss Portia here to draw this agreement up for myself! It only says I'm selling them all rights to the statement I took down at the deathbed of Tim Medicine Dog in Omaha General a few weeks back. There's only one paragraph outlining his last words, and it's agreed I've never said I believed 'em to be anything more than an interesting news item. There isn't anything here they could ever use against us. So let's see some money and I'll be proud to sign in quadruplicate, Counselor!"

Portia shrugged and told Longarm it was his money if he wanted to throw it away on a news item he never meant to see published.

Longarm handed over a hemp paper envelope stuffed with U.S. Treasury silver certificates. Beavergame Banks considered his options, shrugged, and signed.

As he and Swansdown Doris rose, Longarm said, "You are under arrest. The charge is attempted blackmail. We neglected to show you the papers signed by others. We have a night letter signed by Rain Crow of the Indian Police up Montana way to the effect that the late Tim Medicine Dog never worked for Roping Sally, and as likely never *knew* her before he left the reservation to work as a jockey *before I was ever up there*!"

The con man coolly replied, "Then you were right when you called him a liar. I never said anything about any sordid love triangle in Montana Territory. I only took down his dying words in Omaha General and—"

"No you didn't," said Portia Parkhurst, Attorney at Law, with a prim smile, adding, "We have a signed statement from Omaha General Hospital as well. They keep visitors' records in the moribund ward. Neither you nor anyone else took down any last words of the late Tim

8

Medicine Dog. He never recovered consciousness when they brought him to the hospital!"

Beavergame Banks seemed to count to ten under his breath, favored her with a gallant smile, and decided, "Okay, let's call it a Mexican standoff. You get the money back and we agree it's just your word against our own, right?"

"Wrong," said Portia Parkhurst, Attorney at Law, as office furniture began to change position. She introduced the florid-faced fat man who'd been in the corner *behind* that wardrobe as a prosecutor from the State Attorney General's office. The more muscular youth who'd gotten out of that hired hack to hide behind the leather chesterfield was a Captain Wortham of the Colorado State Police.

The heavyset man who'd been hiding all the time under her desk in a derby and checked suit was, of course, Reporter Crawford of the *Denver Post*. He assured them all he'd been taking shorthand notes.

Chapter 2

Swansdown Doris was cussing Beavergame Banks fit to bust as the Colorado lawmen led them away, with Reporter Crawford tagging along to take down every word. Heeding the advice of a good lawyer, Longarm stayed put with Portia in her office suite lest he confuse the police blotter with charges that would likely never stick.

When Longarm had come to her with his more complicated scheme to rid the West for a while of that vicious pair, Portia had pointed out how Swansdown Doris, a simple slut too lazy to work but too self-indulgent to do without, was the weak link they wanted to put some strain on.

Portia had guessed, even before the slick little con man showed up with a witness he usually used to shake down married marks with the old beaver game, that Swansdown Doris, named for a right expensive brand of shimmy shirt silk, would be pissed enough to turn state's evidence when she saw that her con man's efforts at more convoluted blackmail had only gotten her a night or more in a patent cell, facing a year or more on white bread and beans without a puff to powder her nose.

Beavergame Banks's grab for a brighter gold ring than you found in your average transient hotel had been pathetic, and Longarm's very first impulse had been to toss the little shit down a shithouse pit head-first. But Longarm had never cottoned to bullies to begin with, and once he asked around and found out who he was dealing with, he'd seen he'd better put the little shit out of business for a spell.

Beavergame Banks's more usual marks were married men who felt they had more to hide than a knock-around single cuss with the social position of a tumbleweed and an already bad reputation when it came to the ladies.

Their usual beaver game involved Swansdown Doris meeting up with a traveling man on a train or in a hotel lobby, with one thing leading to the other as the night the day, until Banks, as her "Husband!" busted in to catch them in the act, gleefully shouting that he'd caught her at it at last and meant to swear out a bill of divorcement naming this here horny son of a bitch as a home-wrecking correspondent, and so on, until the chump forked over some hush money to just let him put on his pants and run home to his own wife.

Portia had said, and Longarm had agreed, that once the local law had the two of them in separate cells, each anxious to save his or her own skin, it should be simple to get enough on Banks, at least, to put him in Canyon City a spell. Swansdown Doris, left to her own devices on a train or in a hotel lobby, would be more likely to make any traveling man she met feel mighty smug, whether he left anything on the dressing table for her on his way out or not.

So now Portia suggested a drink to their success, but being a woman, as she got out the Napoleon and a couple of snifters, she asked him in a desperately casual tone to tell her more about this Roping Sally from up Montana way, naturally adding, "Was she pretty?"

Accepting his brandy glass as Portia led him over to the chesterfield they'd pushed back in place against the

12

wall, Longarm replied in as desperately casual a tone, "I reckon, if you cotton to big old blondes standing six feet in their Justins. They called her old Roping Sally because she could rope and throw like a top hand. Sat a pony and handled a gun better than most men as well. Like I said, she was this orphan gal raising beef for the Blackfoot Agency."

As they sat down together, Portia said, "Then you really *did* go for her, didn't you. That's about the only thing in your favor, Custis. God knows, you've never been *faithful* to any of us. But unlike all too many men, you really *like* women and *respect* women with intelligence and skill! I could tell you tales about a no-longer-young woman with a law degree from Harvard scaring grown men half to death. But as I recall it, wasn't long after I'd defended a man you'd arrested, and got him off, that you invited me to supper at that silly little Italian restaurant near the federal courts! Was that before or after you'd been in Roping Sally's pantaloons, you old softy?"

Longarm said, "I never told her I'd been in *your* pantaloons. So why should I talk dirty about a murdered lady?"

Portia sipped a whiff of Napoleon and didn't speak for a time. When she did, she said, "You may as well know I sent some wires and asked a few questions of my own as we were setting this trap up, Custis. They say you really did cry before you tracked down and killed both that hired gun who'd killed your Roping Sally and the land-grabbing mastermind he'd been working for!"

Longarm tried some of the fancy French brandy. It smelled better than it tasted. He leaned back and told Portia, "I wish I could make that brag. I can't. I got to run a train over the one as murdered old Roping Sally. The Land Office bigwig he'd been working for died from the combined effects of bullets and battery acid, administered

13

by another crook I did get to shoot. But I wasn't half as sore at *him*!"

Portia snuggled closer to murmur, "If somebody murdered me, Custis, would you cry real tears and splash him with battery acid for me?"

He put his free arm around her, sensing she wanted him to, as he replied, "I reckon. I've yet to see you rope and throw, but you're right about my admiring smart women who can *do* things. Things less natural than most women know how to do, I mean. I know some men cotton most to beautiful but dumb gals, and I'll allow there are times I'd as soon a gal would shut up and kiss me. But I fear I just ain't man enough to play slap-and-tickle hour after hour with a pretty gal, and there do come times, between times, when a gent feels like *talking* with a cell mate, and Lord have mercy, it do get tedious talking about Paris frocks and whether Queen Victoria really sleeps with her butler or not!"

As he set aside his snifter to run that hand under her black poplin, Portia gleeped, "Not here! Not this early during business hours, silly! What if somebody comes?"

He said coming was what he had in mind.

She got rid of her own snifter to grab his bigger wrist in both her hands before it was too late, protesting, "Not in this office on this chesterfield, Custis! I mean it! Let me up so I can hang my OUT ON A CASE sign in the hall and lock the damned door!"

Longarm didn't argue. He was glad he hadn't, a few moments later, when she led him through the empty meeting room next to her reception area, and thence into yet another inner chamber he hadn't known about up until then.

He'd just told her he admired gals who had interesting things to say or new truths to reveal when a man wasn't actually on top of them.

Then Portia Parkhurst, Attorney at Law, revealed the

day bed she kept made up for emergencies in her downtown office, and Longarm was on top of her in no time as she wriggled and giggled about it being no later than nine outside, for heaven's sake.

It was a caution how lean and hungry-built gals with big tits could treat a poor old boy at nine in the morning once you got them out of a severe black business suit to do it right with no more than a black velvet band around their white throats and black high-buttons covering their trim ankles, aimed in every direction but the floor.

Stark naked, Portia Parkhurst, Attorney at Law, sort of reminded Longarm of a firmly padded ironing board with a couple of grapefruit halves for a man to recline his bare chest against. But he could come up with no analogy for what felt like the pure ring-dang-doo of a natural woman between Portia's lean but shapely thighs.

She seemed to feel his old organ grinder felt natural enough as he slithered it in and out of her while somewhere out front, the twist-doorbell of her front office was ringing fit to bust.

Portia sighed, "I *told* you these were business hours, you sex maniac! It will serve me right if they take a juicy case to another lawyer in this very building!"

Longarm suggested she might answer through the door to come back later as he just lay low.

Portia sighed and said, "The way a certain widow woman up in Sherman did that weekend you spent with her?"

Longarm didn't answer.

Portia smiled like Miss Mona Lisa in that print and said soothingly, "Don't worry, stud. Your secret is safe with me. Or it would be if everybody in Denver didn't know about you and that young mine-owning widow. I know better than to offer excuses. That's why everybody in Denver doesn't know about you and me. I hope. We'll just lie still, and in a little bit they'll give up, take their business elsewhere, and we can make all the noise back here we want."

So sure enough, the pestiferous ringing finally stopped, and they felt free to do it again, Portia being noisier than he was at such times.

But such times lasted such a little while when you considered how many less delightful times you were stuck with in an average lifetime. So, as a clock struck ten A.M. somewhere in the sunny distance, they wound up sharing a smoke, stark naked atop the covers and glad of it as an August sun rose ever higher outside.

As Portia snuggled her partly unbound head against Longarm's bare shoulder while he smoked himself saner, he found himself compelled to say, "That con man never got away with them marked treasury bills after all, and like he said, I came by the money by sheer luck whilst I was out in the field. So about that retainer you refused when I first came to you about them blackmailers . . ."

"Forget it," she said. "I told you then I'd heard about that pair and their nastly little badger game. I'm a for-Chrissake paid-up member of the courthouse gang, and more than one of their other marks has been pleading in vain for somebody, anybody, to do something about Beavergame Banks that wouldn't involve their own testimony in an open court. So my public-spirited entrapment of that pair will go down well for this girl around Courthouse Square in the days to come."

Longarm took a thoughtful drag on their three-for-a-nickel cheroot and said, "I still wish there was some way Roping Sally and me could pay you back. Like I told you earlier, they picked the wrong horse when they thought I'd pay to protect the rep of an orphan gal who died respected by all the neighbors up Montana way. But thanks to you, they don't even get to *lie* about poor old Roping Sally."

16

"Oh, come on, you know you fucked her, Custis!" the naked woman in his arms insisted.

Longarm said, "I don't want to talk about that part. They lied when they said a busted-up rider who never woke up from a bad fall said I took her away from him. She never had no full-time hands, red or white, working for her small spread when I was up that way. It's as likely Tim Medicine Dog never knew her at all, let alone in a Biblical sense."

He caught himself just in time, and never added that Roping Sally had been a virgin before he'd misunderstood her innocently crawling into bed with him that time, to *his* chagrin but to their mutual delight, before that shit-eating dog Yardbull Mendez cut her up just awful. So he quit while he was ahead by adding, "Suffice it to say, nobody I knew up Montana way will appear in the *Denver Post*'s coverage of their arrest, and so, like I said, I feel I owe you, Miss Portia."

She twiddled his limp dick thoughtfully as she conceded, "Well, I have another friend in a fix just north of the Colorado line if you have any leave time coming."

Longarm grimaced and explained, "I'm paid day rates plus expenses and a small bonus each time I make an arrest or serve a court order out in the field. If I want to take a few days off, without pay, my boss may go for it unless he has something better for me to do. So tell me more about this other gent you know up Wyoming way."

She laughed and assured him she'd never ask a lover to pull another lover's nuts out of the fire. She added, "It's a girl I went through law school with. Her name is Tess Hayward. We came West together after graduation. As you know and we found out the hard way, a woman can own property and practice law in Colorado, but as yet she can't vote or run for public office. Tess took that harder than I did once I got the chance to buy this practice from an older worn-out male."

Longarm blew a thoughtful smoke ring and decided, "I'd be sore if I was a gal too. So your law school classmate hung her shingle out up Wyoming way, and then what?"

Portia said, "After she'd won big for the Stock Growers Association and made friends with the Grange, winning some pro bono cases for small holders, Tess ran for District Attorney of Buffalo Ford, a few hours down Crow Creek from Cheyenne, and won big some more. Buffalo Ford was a lawless cow town when Tess took over and tamed the dickens out of it four years ago."

"All by her dainty self?" asked Longarm as he twiddled a nipple between thumb and forefinger.

Portia said, "Not so hard, damn it! Do you like it when I pinch your dick like *this*? Tess naturally works with honest county courts, and got rid of their crooked town marshal. The boys she replaced the old bunch with are devoted to her. They run the wilder element in, and Tess sees they consider the error of their ways on the county road gang unless they'd care to just leave town and never come back again."

Longarm said, "I get the picture. What's her problem if she has her town so tame these days?"

Portia moved his hand to a more intimate part of her anatomy as she explained, "This November. It's an election year and she's running real scared, Custis."

He asked, "How come? If she's done such a good job, she ought to win in a walk. Who's she got running against her for control of a bitty cow town for Pete's sake?"

Portia said, "I think she said his name is Wilcox. They call him Big Dick Wilcox, but it isn't funny. According to Tess, he has no law degree and the ethics of an Algerian rug merchant. But he's got money. A lot of money. He's a big spender at the dozen saloons in town, and worse yet, generous to widows and orphans in a show-off way. You know the type?"

Longarm said, "Yep. You call 'em politicians. That's how they get elected when they have nothing else to offer. I feel for your friend, Town-Taming Tess. But I don't see what anyone can do for her. Buying your way into public office is the American way."

Then, as he felt Portia Parkhurst, Attorney at Law, going cold and stiff in his arms, Longarm said soothingly, "Don't get sore. I said I didn't see what anyone could do for her. But I told you earlier that I owed you. So cuddle up a little closer and let me see if I can come up with anything that might possibly work!"

Chapter 3

They couldn't. They'd sprung their trap on a Saturday morn and so, the courts and most government offices having closed early by the time they got up, they had a lazy afternoon, a Saturday night complete with yet another supper at Romano's, and the whole Sabbath over at Portia's quarters to plot the ruination of Big Dick Wilcox, the would-be district attorney of the dinky cow town Portia's pal had seen first.

Portia couldn't seem to get it through her severely pretty head that baby-kissing cocksuckers with more money almost always won elections because a majority of voters were poor and stupid.

Portia protested, "Women are allowed to vote in local elections up in Wyoming, Custis. Don't you think that might help poor Tess?"

To which he could only reply, "Most women in a dinky cow town are poor and stupid to spare or they'd be somewheres else. Majority rule is the fatal flaw in a democracy. The majority will almost always go with the bigger smile, bigger promises, and an occasional round of drinks."

Portia asked what form of government Longarm preferred, in that case. He answered simply, "Democracy. It's

21

the only game in town, crooked as it may be. The only form of government with a Chinaman's chance of working as advertised would be an autocracy run by a good-natured genius the way they say Heaven, Rome under the few good emperors, or the Papist church under outstanding popes is alleged to work. Once you let the *politicians* run anything, you get an awful mess, and democracy usually turns out least awful. Dictators, kings, and sometimes I wonder about gods, are inclined to get arrogant as all get-out when they don't have to worry about pulling the wool over the voters' eyes."

Portia sighed. "Poor Tess writes that Big Dick Wilcox already has every drunken bum in town drinking to him and the election's less than four months away. I don't suppose it would be right for somebody to just go up yonder and *shoot* the rascal."

Longarm told her you called *that* form of government anarchy. So they put their heads together some more, and that felt so good they put some other parts together, and that felt even better, although it failed to inspire any grand notions about the coming November elections.

So Longarm was still wracking his brains on behalf of Town-Taming Tess Hayward when he got to the Federal Building on a cold gray Monday morn, walking funny after such an athletic weekend.

As he entered the outer offices of Marshal William Vail of the Denver District Court, old Henry, the young squirt they had playing the typewriter up front, favored Longarm with one of his knowing "Now-you're-going-to-get-it!" smiles and said, "We missed you Satuday morning, Deputy Long. Were you getting drunk, getting laid, or both?"

Longarm smiled as knowingly and replied, "Don't knock either before you try them, Henry. Boss in the back?"

"And anxious to see you the moment you might remember you're working here, *if* you're still working here," Henry sniffed.

So Longarm headed back through their office suite, lighting a cheroot along the way in self-defense. Longarm had heard Billy Vail's wife nagging him about the way his duds reeked of tobacco smoke. Longarm suspected the crusty old cuss smoked his fool self like a ham with all the windows shut to get back at her remarks about his expensive but awesomely pungent cigars.

Longarm entered the older lawman's inner sanctum, braced for an ass-chewing about Saturday morn. But fortunately for Longarm, and even Town-Taming Tess, news of the arrest at Lawyer Parkhurst's had beaten Longarm to work that Monday morn.

Waving Longarm to a seat in the battered leather guest chair across from his cluttered desk, the older, shorter, and way stockier Billy Vail said, "You done us proud, old son. The party boys I drink with at the club were so pleased with us, it was all I could do to keep 'em from noticing I didn't know what they were talking about as I modestly took the credit due me for having such a slick senior deputy. It seems that little shit who tried to shake you down has done better, milking others who gave more of a shit about their reputations."

Leaning back in his swivel chair, Vail went on. "Just as your slick female lawyer suggested to the State of Colorado, Swansdown Doris wrote and signed a full confession, blaming her confederate for steering a good girl who never meant no harm down the primrose path. They'll be letting her off with time served, once they shove the umbrella up his ass and open it. Don't never shake down a state senator if you figure on spending much time in the same state!"

Vail chuckled and added, "Of course, since the senator never gives his right name to broads he picks up in the Tremont lobby, Beavergame Banks never knew what a

23

big fish they'd caught until you caught *them*, you rascal, and I'm so pleased with you I aim to let you out of that courtroom duty you despise so for a whole week!"

Longarm grabbed for the brass ring, saying, "I was only doing my job. But seeing I have you in such a good mood, and seeing we owe the arrest that's made you so popular to Portia Parkhurst, I got a favor for a friend of hers to ask you, Boss."

You could see the pane of bullet-proof caution slide into place between them as Billy Vail told Longarm he was listening.

By the time Longarm had outlined the situation up Wyoming way, the older lawman looked less tense. His voice was almost gentle as he told Longarm, "I reckon we can spare you for a week, seeing we owe Lawyer Parkhurst, and with the understanding you'll be on your own time and won't get to charge expenses to this office. I suppose there's no need to tell a man with your experience in government work that he's on his way to Wyoming to tilt at windmills like old Don Quixote, eh?"

Longarm shrugged and said, "I told Miss Portia I'd try. I don't know how many windmills I can take on in just one week, though. So I don't suppose you could make that *two* weeks?"

Vail's voice was less gentle as he shook his bullet head and snapped at Longarm, "Don't push your luck with this child, Deputy Long! We both know that unless your Big Dick Wilcox turns out to be wanted federal, there ain't a thing you can do to him in two weeks or *six* weeks that you can't manage in one, seeing you insist on going through the motions for a pretty lawyer."

When he saw Longarm knew better than to argue, Vail added in a more fatherly tone, "Why don't you just hop a Burlington local as far up as Cheyenne, try changing your luck along Crow Creek, and . . . Oh, shit, Miss Portia's likely to wire her district attorney pal you're on your

24

way. So, *bueno,* see how bad things are for her up yonder, and come back to tell Miss Portia there wasn't a thing you could do. I don't see why any woman who ain't hideously deformed would want a man's job to start with."

Longarm agreed it was likely the contrary nature of the unfair sex, and lit out with Billy Vail's blessings to see if he could save Town-Taming Tess Hayward's manly job for her.

He had to go home to his hired digs on the unfashionable side of old Cherry Creek first.

Unlike the famous lawmen in Ned Buntline's Wild West magazines, he didn't support a horse full-time on his modest pay. But he had a well-broken-in McClellan Army saddle to ride aboard such mounts he might borrow or hire for an occasional field mission far from the remuda the office boarded in a Denver livery near the Federal Building.

The old cavalry saddle, designed more for the comfort of the horse than the rider, came with brass fittings to hold more shit than your average horse could carry. Longarm contented himself with saddlebags and a bedroll keeping company with the saddle boot of his Winchester '73, chambered for the same .44-40 rounds as his double-action Colt.

Seeing he'd be backing the play of a public official up in Buffalo Ford, Longarm undressed to travel more comfortably, but packed the three-piece suit of tobacco tweed they expected a lawman to wear around fool courtrooms under the Hayes Reform Administration. He hauled on clean but faded jeans, a hickory shirt, and a denim jacket as bleached by the sun, wind, and rain as the jeans. He replaced the sissy shoestring tie he wore around the Federal Building with a knotted bandanna, strapped his crossdraw rig back around his slender hips, and filled the pockets of his denim outfit with the shit from the pockets of the suit, including an accurate enough pocket watch with a double derringer clipped to the other end of its gold watch chain.

After that, there was nothing much left to do but get on up to Buffalo Ford by way of Cheyenne. It wasn't such a long walk by way of the Larimer Street Bridge to Union Station, where, sure enough, a northbound day tripper gave him barely time to stock up on extra smokes and some reading material. Experienced travelers knew better than to buy any reading material off the candy butchers working the trains between stops.

Noting he still had twenty minutes to kill, and seeing the Western Union next to the waiting room wasn't busy, Longarm sashayed in to tear off a yellow blank, address it to Portia's nearby office, and write in block letters, "ON WAY STOP CUSTIS," for it cost the same nickel a word whether Western Union delivered your message in New York City or just across the street, and he figured his twenty cents worth would assure old Portia as well as six bits worth might have.

Then he got himself and his load aboard the club car of the northbound day tripper, and ordered a schooner of lager before the train started. The morning was shaping up warm by the time they were out of the yards and moving north across the rolling swells of open range. So he ordered another.

There wasn't much else a sensible traveler could do aboard a day tripper bound from Denver to Cheyenne. The tedious trip lasted four or five hours, thanks to all the pestiferous local stops, so there was no sense wondering whether that auburn-headed little thing in the calico Rainy Susie skirts wanted to know why the city of Cheyenne they were bound for made Mister Lo, the Poor Indian, snicker.

Had there been time, he'd have bought her another planter's punch if that suited her better than beer, and explained how, as usual, the white man had named a whole town after an Indian nickname.

"Cheyenne" was the French Canadian spelling of "Sha-hi'yenah," or "people who talk funny" in the lingo of their Lakota allies. They called their fool *selves* "Tsitsissah." But what the hell, Sioux City was named after what their Ojibwa enemies called the Lakota. So it worked out sort of fair when one considered how many Tsitsissah lived in Cheyenne or how many Lakota, Dakota, or even Nakota lived in Sioux City.

As all things good and bad must, the tedious run up to Cheyenne was over at last by high noon, and Longarm had only *thought* he was being sensible about that gal in the Rainy Susie skirts until he heard his name being paged as he lugged his heavily laden saddle into the Union Station they'd built up in Cheyenne. When the porter who'd scouted him up led him out front where District Attorney Tess Hayward sat holding the reins of her oilcloth-topped surrey, Longarm felt so sensible he wanted to hug his fool self.

For the first thing he learned upon meeting up with a classmate of Portia Parkhurst was how he'd been right all along about Portia starting to go gray prematurely. Tess Hayward, who'd gone through law school with Portia, looked to be ten years younger, though he figured she had to be in her thirties when she'd first run for public office, four years back.

After that, as he put his load on the rear seat and climbed up beside her, Longarm saw that Town-Taming Tess filled her summer-weight mint-green bodice with a good ten or fifteen pounds more than, bony Portia. Tess Hayward, in sum, was built like a brick shithouse.

Her face wasn't tough to take either. Like her colleague down in Denver, the freckled towhead wore her hair in a severe bun, with a stern expression to go with it. Longarm warned himself not to wonder when he wondered whether, like her severe-looking classmate Portia, Town-Taming Tess looked a lot less severe when she was coming in a man's arms.

He offered to take the reins, of course. She sounded defensive as she demurred, "I guess I know the way better than you, ah . . . Custis. I drove up from Buffalo Ford as soon as I got Portia's wire about you being on your way to run Big Dick Wilcox out of town!"

Idly wondering what else Portia might have told an old school chum about him, Longarm soberly replied, "I ain't certain I can promise you as much as that, Miss Tess. I have some wires of my own out, and there just might be something, somewhere, on a police blotter or mayhaps in a bankruptcy court file. But I wouldn't bank on either. Miss Portia tells me he's been outspending you on the campaign trail?"

As she snapped the ribbons against the rump of her one cordovan mule, Tess sighed, "I wasn't planning on putting up posters this side of mid-September. It's just not *fair* for a total stranger to horn into my town like so and throw money about as if he has to spend it before the ink can dry! He never warned me he was after my *job* before he'd dug himself in as a good old boy, ready to stand a round of drinks any time or bail out a crying woman's likkered-up man! He never said toad squat about wanting anyone to vote for him when he organized the best Fourth of July picnic and fireworks show Buffalo Ford had ever seen!"

Longarm didn't ask why they were headed south toward Crow Creek. She had just told him she knew where they were headed. The map allowed that the town of Buffalo Ford, like Cheyenne itself, lay on the banks of the same Crow Creek. He figured asking if they'd named her town after a stretch of Crow Creek buffalo had once been prone to cross would be a dumb question. So he asked if she had any notion why a big spender might blow into a remote cow town, no offense, and start buying up votes with, what? His own money?

Tess sighed and said, "My own friends and me have tried in vain to hook Big Dick Wilcox up with the Republicans, the Democrats, the Grange, or even the Red Flaggers. He seems to be acting on his own, like a rich kid out to buy himself a grown-up title. He's not *fit* to be a district attorney, Custis! I'm a member of the Wyoming Bar Association, and they have no record of him ever practicing law at any level, anywhere!"

Longarm said, "Miss Portia told me you're in good with the Stock Growers Association and the Grange as well as your own party machine, Miss Tess?"

She said, "I thought I was. But all the men I've turned to up this way, up to now, keep telling me Big Dick Wilcox has every right to run for any public office and there's nothing they can do about it!"

To which Longarm could have only replied, "Amen!"

So he didn't say anything as they turned east to follow the creek-side wagon trace.

Chapter 4

Crow Creek and the Union Pacific tracks departed from Cheyenne close enough together for the bawling cows of a passing freight to spook their mule. Longarm admired the way Tess steadied it, putting her trim back into the effort. They'd already established she was a gal used to being in control of situations.

The driving got less spooky as they trended east-southeast, with the creek and railroad diverging slowly but steadily. Longarm couldn't come up with much that didn't sound mighty flattering. So he didn't ask how come a boss lady with a legal staff, a town marshal, and his deputies at her disposal had chosen to drive into Cheyenne alone to meet his train. Western Union wouldn't let you send dirty words along its wires. But old school chums had ways of fixing one another up with secret codes.

But if good old Portia was that good a sport about her love life, Town-Taming Tess didn't seem to act like she was out to seduce him. So he asked if she had any notion why her one cow town might hold more attraction than others scattered across the High Plains for any real spenders out to buy themselves an election.

Tess said, "I've studied that blue in the face, and none

31

of the men I know who know more than me about grazing this north range have been able to hazard a guess! Grass is grass to a cow, and while the open range around Buffalo Ford offers yummy blue grama and bunchgrass for the grazing, so do townships in every direction. It can't be water rights Big Dick or any secret backers could be after. Any stockman out to claim water rights along Crow Creek could do so cheaper along many an unclaimed and un-occupied mile! Crow Creek winds across better than forty miles of mostly open Wyoming range before it dips below the Colorado line to wend its way for sixty or so down to the South Platte!"

Longarm said, "I noticed. Me and Miss Portia were studying the map together over the weekend. Crow Creek joins the bigger South Platte and smaller Cache La Poudre in the middle of nowheres much, east of Greeley, Colo-rado. What about mineral claims up this way? I know you don't find *color* in prairie creeks this far east of the moun-tains. But a spell back we caught a slicker trying to corner coal, natural gas, and rock oil rights way down deep under alluvial soil."

Tess said, "Give a girl with a college degree credit for knowing where to look in the library stacks back yonder, Custis! There are no, repeat, no coal measures or oil seeps this side of the Laramies, and they've yet to find anything richer than iron ore in the Laramies. The Union Pacific stokes its cross-country trains on Wyoming coal, and if there was any worth digging as close to their right of way as Buffalo Ford, they'd have surely found it!"

Before Longarm could reply, she added, "I'm not guessing. I'm telling. I have friends of my own persuasion married to railroad officials who prospect for engine coal within reach of their operations!"

She'd told Longarm more than that. Portia Parkhurst had told him, and she kept confirming, she had Wyoming connections in high places, not to mention she was smart

32

as a whip and pretty as a picture. So what in thunder had inspired this Big Dick Wilcox, or the bunch he might be fronting for, to choose Town-Taming Tess as an easy target?

He asked her permission to smoke, lit up, and as they rode along, asked her about any feuds or range wars down the trace ahead. She told him, "As a matter of fact things have been mighty peaceful for the last two years or more. Had a little trouble restoring law and order, as I'd promised I would, when I first took over. But as bad as it was when I ousted the pathetic political hack pretending to be a D.A., we never had anything serious enough to call a *range war* over in Buffalo Ford! Why do you ask?"

Longarm replied, "My boss calls it the process of eliminating. How about robberies—railroad, post road, or in town?"

She said, "We've had some *theft* in and about Buffalo Ford. Nothing violent as armed robbery since I've been in office. The toughest nuts to crack are wife-beating drunks. Can't get their wives to press charges and can't get *them* to stop drinking. What are you driving at, Custis?"

He enjoyed a thoughtful drag before he told her, "Eliminating. If they ain't out to take over your town for some reason, they're out to take over your *job,* see?"

She said, "No. So far, this one summer, Big Dick has spent more than my yearly salary."

Longarm nodded and declared, "Meaning it's the *position,* not the usual salary of an honest D.A., the big spender's after!"

She muttered, "Thanks. I never would have figured that a man out to beat me at the polls come November might be after my *job. Of course* the carpetbagging big spender is after my job!"

"Why?" Longarm insisted. "There's always a why, unless we assume a lunatic with lots of money always wanted to be the district attorney of a cow town when he grew up. So I got me a sort of fuzzy picture forming in the mists ahead. But I'll be switched with snakes if I see any motive for Lincoln County moves."

"Lincoln what?" she demanded.

He said, "That war they had down New Mexico way for control of the Lincoln County beef and retail trade. It ended bad for all concerned, and the newpapers ever since have reported the confusion all wrong. But the local D.A., or in this case U.S. Attorney Thomas Catron, who had much the same duties under the territorial misrule of the Santa Fe Ring, was the key player few newspaper reporters ever mention."

Tess reined in to steady her mule as a tumbleweed crossed the wagon trace ahead. As the tense moment passed, she said, "Now that you mention it, I have read some articles about that Lincoln County War. That was the one with Billy the Kid on one side and some bigwig's hired guns on the other, right?"

Longarm said, "Wrong. Billy Bonney or Henry McCarty, depending on who you ask, was a tagalong kid with a memorable nickname riding under the leadership of the late Dick Brewer. Brewer in turn rode for the ill-advised Chisum, MacSween, and Tunstall faction. Protestant outsiders who tried to horn in on Irish Catholic Union vets who'd carved out a good thing for themselves selling beef to the Army and B.I.A. and dry goods to the mostly Mex local *rancheros*."

"What has all that got to do with an outsider trying to horn in on *me,* for heaven's sake?" she demanded.

Longarm said, "Uncle John Chisum was an unreconstructed Texas Rebel who convinced a Canadian named MacSween and a Londoner named Tunstall they had a fighting chance against the Murphy, Dolan, Ryan, and Brady bunch. They could see Major Murphy had Sheriff Brady in his hip pocket. So after some of Brady's deputies

34

gunned down the green-as-grass young Tunstall, the survivors gunned the sheriff instead of running whilst the running was good."

He let that sink in, then explained, "Owning the town law or even the county sheriff is nothing next to owning the lawyers who get to say whether there might be a *trial* or not, depending on just how a charge might read. Being furriners, MacSween and Tunstall had figured it meant beans if they could wrangle *badges* for their own hired guns. You being a law school graduate, do I have to detail how things went down Lincoln County way with the U.S. Attorney, the U.S. Army, and the Bureau of Indian Affairs backing the county machine the outsiders had declared war against?"

Tess nodded knowingly and replied, "I wish Big Dick Wilcox would come at me that crudely. My town marshal, owing his own job to my good offices, has assured me he'll pistol-whip, gutshoot, and then *kill* any outside troublemakers he can catch in the act of spitting on the boardwalk. I can picture how an inside clique of Union vets must have felt about a Texas Reb and his fresh young pards down in Lincoln County. But *they* were dumb enough to give the established machine an excuse to fight back the easy way! My backers and me just don't have the unlimited funds to fight Big Dick's way!"

He said, "Nobody has unlimited funds, Miss Tess. And it's often darkest before the dawn. So for all we know, your unworthy rival could be already scraping the bottoms of his pockets."

"What if he has enough, just enough, to outspend me this side of, say, Halloween?" she asked.

Longarm knew she didn't want to hear you had to know when to fold 'em. Dick Brewer, Sandy MacSween, and John Tunstall had no doubt been offered such advice and chosen to ignore it.

They talked some more in circles, and then Tess turn

off the wagon trace just short of what seemed a middling town up ahead. When he saw they'd turned into the door-yard of a whitewashed frame cottage, he was able to refrain from dumb questions until, sure enough, Tess Hayward told him it was her place and added, "I didn't tell anybody in town when Portia wired you were coming. Not even my friends. I thought you might want to sort of work in secret until you got something on that horrid Big Dick! Portia tells me you can be awfully sneaky!"

Longarm stared at her incredulously, and started to ask what the sneakiest of sneaks might uncover about a big spender spending lawfully in plain sight. But as he got down first to take the ribbons and help her down, Long-arm reflected on the slight edge a pussyfoot into town as an unknown quality might offer.

He declared, "The usual form requires a visiting law-man to pay a courtesy call on the local peace officers. But on the other hand, I'm on my own time and so this ain't an official visit yet. Why don't you warm up some coffee whilst I put this rolling stock and your mule away in yon carriage house, ma'am? It's early for pussyfooting, and I could use some black coffee ahead of time if I mean to mosey into your town after dark unannounced."

So she told him to join her in her kitchen by way of her back door as soon as they were shed of her rolling stock and livestock. She intimated she'd have something better than just coffee waiting for him.

But Longarm took his time and did a decent job over in her carriage house. He unhitched her mule and led it by its halter into the empty stall next to the one occupied by a nervous paint mare. He got the bit out of the mule's mouth as soon as he'd rubbed it dry with a handy burlap feed sack. Then he made certain both critters had water as well as cracked corn in their mangers before he secured their stalls and hauled the surrey inside to occupy most of such space as there still was. As he shut the bottom leaf of the double door, he glanced up at the sky, wrinkled his nose, and hauled out his pocket watch to mutter, "Shit, it won't be dark for hours and pretty as she may be, I've about talked Big Dick Wilcox more than once around the same circles!"

Walking slowly across the backyard toward the open invitation of her kitchen door, Longarm sighed, "Damn it to hell, Miss Tess, I just can't rightly *say* why anybody would want your job enough to treat the whole blamed town to free drinks and fireworks!"

Joining her in her cozy-smelling kitchen, Longarm saw the shapely towheaded Tess had laid out a swell spread of hot coffee and cold meats on the deal table near the eastward-facing open window. He saw she'd changed into a robe of cream Turkish toweling, and slippers with big yellow pom-poms as well. Imperious gals who lived alone as their own bosses got used to dressing as they damn well pleased in warm weather, he had to assume.

Setting his Stetson aside before he sat down at the table, Longarm said, "I left my saddle and Winchester out in your carriage house, Miss Tess. I'm still working on whether I ought to just walk on in afoot or borrow that saddle pony of yours. There's much to be said for either approach."

She said she'd be proud to loan him her Spanky Girl, but added she didn't follow his drift.

He dug in to build himself a ham and cheese on rye as he explained, "I wear these low-heeled cavalry stovepipes because I have found it sometimes pays to be light on one's feet. If I just walk on in, I'll have no tethered bronc out front to worry about if I decide to vanish a lot. On the other hand, a stranger appearing out of nowheres, afoot, can inspire heaps of questions in your average cow town."

She nodded and sat across from him to suggest, "What if you waited until well after supper time, when it's good

37

and dark on the streets of Buffalo Ford and the saloon doors have been swinging some? Would anybody marvel at a quiet man dressed like a cowboy in your average cow town, Custis?''

He decided, "Likely not, and I doubt I'll have much use for a saddle gun unless I can get Big Dick to confess right off he's wanted in the County of Clay for robbing that Glendale train.''

He washed some grub down with black coffee and consulted his watch again before he said, "Cow towns don't come to life after dark much earlier than nine, so we sure have us some time to kill with the sun still up outside.''

She said, "We'll think of something. Would you like some marble cake before we make ourselves more comfortable up front?''

Longarm confessed he'd been nibbling like a time-killing mouse all the way up from Denver, and added, "I wanted your swell black coffee to keep me awake and on my toes in town this evening. I take it you want me to hide out here with you later tonight, unless I manage to get myself invited to join Big Dick's gang?''

She said she'd ridden alone to meet him with just such skullduggery in mind, and suggested he bring his cup of coffee along if he cared to.

He left the almost empty cup on the table, and rose to follow as she led the way down a short hallway and thence into what surely looked and smelled like a lady's boudoir. He managed not to bleat like a moon calf, but it wasn't easy as Town-Taming Tess turned to face him, by her four-poster, to let her robe fall away from her stark-naked charms.

One of the first things he naturally noticed was that she was towheaded all over.

He took a deep breath and let half of it out so his voice wouldn't crack as he soberly observed, "I reckon our mu-

38

tual pal, Lawyer Portia Parkhurst, must have told some secrets out of school!"

To which she calmly replied, "She did indeed. But frankly, I have my doubts about her bragging. So why don't you take off those clothes and prove you're half the stud she told me you were."

Chapter 5

From the way she carried on aboard that four-poster with Longarm atop her and the two pillows under her rolicking rump, he seemed to be living up to the promises made to one old school chum by another. He never asked how long the two lawyer gals had been hunting in pairs. He'd established back in Denver that Portia was mighty fond of old Tess, and he suspected that had Portia been there with them that long lazy afternoon, the two discreetly lusty lawyers might have come up with some mighty shocking positions. Gals didn't worry half as much as gents about being considered queer.

So they enjoyed such queer positions as they could manage without a third party, and if she was telling the truth, he made her come seven times before she suddenly commenced to bawl like a baby and bury her red face in the pillows, sobbing, "You know damned well!" when he asked what was eating her for Gawd's sake.

So he found his shirt on the rug near the bed and fished out a smoke to light, sitting on the edge of the bed with his bare ass turned to her pulchritude as it heaved with moans and groans about how lonely it was at the top.

When he just went on smoking for a spell, Tess

41

propped herself up on one elbow and protested, "I'm not the slut you take me for! I don't know what got into me just now! How could I have said such dirty things and asked a man I hardly knew to use me and abuse me so?"

Since she'd asked, Longarm quietly observed, "What got into you just now is called my old organ grinder in more polite circles, or a horny old cock in others. I have already had this dumb conversation with a mutual horny friend of ours. I told her I understood how a lady with natural feelings and an unnatural position to uphold in a man's world might go months all prim and proper, only to go *loca en la cabeza,* or in point of fact betwixt her legs, on such rare occasions as she may feel safe to act natural. There ain't no shame in acting a mite wild at such times, Miss Tess. It takes a *real* slut to just lay there not caring whilst she's getting properly fucked."

Tess gasped, "Don't say that word! Can't you see I feel humiliated enough and . . . Oh, my God! Was that really me begging you to fuck me, fuck me, fuck me while you were, dear Lord, *fucking* me?"

Longarm replied, "I was too busy enjoying myself to pay much mind to our conversation, no offense. Would you care for a drag on this cheroot, seeing you already feel so depraved?"

She laughed sheepishly, and reached for the cheroot as she confessed she'd always wondered if it was true about those French gals puffing a cigar with their you-know-whats.

Longarm suggested she give the notion a try. She blushed like a rose and gasped, "I couldn't! Not even if I was alone!"

Then she laughed sort of crazy, and damned if she *couldn't* get the tip of that cheroot to wink red off and on with the other end parting the near-white thatch between her drawn-up thighs. He'd already noticed her thighs were way bigger and softer-looking than old Portia's. She laughed like a mean little kid and said, "I know exactly what you're thinking, Mr. Know-it-all! You think I got elected to my office by sleeping with all the members of the Wyoming Stock Growers Association, don't you?"

"Well, not all of 'em," he answered gallantly.

Town-Taming Tess whipped the lit cheroot out of her twat and threw it at him. As it landed on the shag rug near his jeans, Longarm dove for it, muttering, "Set your house afire if you've a mind to, but spare the only comfortable duds I brung along, dad blast it!"

She asked in a worried childish tone if this meant he didn't want to help her win the November election after all.

Longarm said, "I can't stay up this way till November. I was lucky to get a week off. As to whether I still feel honor-bound to investigate a possible election fraud or not, Miss Tess, I promised Miss Portia I would before I ever knew you, in the Biblical sense or any other. Like I was saying before, there's business and there's pleasure. I try to keep 'em separate in my skull. If this Big Dick Wilcox is up to anything dirty, I mean to put a stop to it. If he ain't, I can't, whether the two of us act dirty or not. So do you want to get dirty on top, seeing we still have some gloaming light to work with afore I head in to town?"

She proved more than willing. As it kept getting darker, Tess got to talking and wriggling wilder. He'd noticed other natural gals with natural feelings, raised on tight reins under rules set by old Queen Victoria, seemed to burst a dam of pent-up dreams and forbidden notions as soon as they let themselves go in the arms of an understanding cuss.

He studied on that as he headed into town well after dark, wearing his official store-bought tweed suit, with his Stetson worn neither cocky nor timid, and the grips of his six-gun under the tail of his coat.

43

Her repeated insistance that she hadn't screwed any-body else on her way to public office was as good as a confession that she had, and a naturally warm-natured woman who never used her warm nature to get ahead was not by definition a natural woman.

Old Professor Darwin had suggested, and Longarm had no call to disagree, that everybody's female ancestors, all the way back to old Mother Eve, had screwed smarter than their dumber sisters who'd screwed dumb and left no fit survivors. Longarm figured it was only fair when gals fighting their way up in a man's world took such help as they could get from men who wanted to screw them. He knew he'd have been unlikely to give a gnat's fart about the coming elections if it hadn't been for one gal he'd screwed asking him to help another gal he'd just screwed. But he was dammit *missing* something here!

Tess Hayward was a competent lawyer who'd won of-fice one way or the other, and had all the advantages of incumbency and no doubt a few mighty close friends in the Stock Growers Association, along with the Grange and her party machine. Therefore, she was about the last dug-in D.A. any rank outsider without a law degree had a lick of business tangling with!

As he ambled on into what was little more than a wide spot in a north-south cattle trail where it crossed a non-descript prairie creek, Longarm could see how any real spender, or somebody fronting for a big-spending syndi-cate, could *build* themselves a town impressive as Buffalo Ford for a few dollars more!

Like so many others scattered across the north range, Buffalo Ford was mostly sun-silvered softwood siding on balloon-frame construction.

To Longarm's relief, there were only half-a-dozen oil-fired streetlamps widely scattered along the north-south main street. More light spilled out the front glass and batwing doors of the five old-time saloons, one wine theater, and a right noisy card house with a bar and free-lunch counter along one wall. Other business establishments such as the one smithy, two hardwares, and a drugstore had shut down for the night, of course. But lamplight outlining a wooden Indian said a dinky tobacco shop was still open. So Longarm moseyed in to buy some cheroots. A man could always use another cheroot, and like barbers, small-town tobacconists heard all the local gossip.

The old-timer inside was a red-bearded man with a Scotch burr. Longarm managed not to say he'd heard tobacco shops had been invented by Scots, or that the first wooden Indian had been a Highland laddy. For nobody liked an asshole who told you what you already knew.

From the easygoing way the old-timer served a strange face, it seemed safe to assume the locals were not on the prod for strange faces. As he pocketed his change, Longarm casually allowed he'd just come over from nearby Cheyenne. When the local shopkeeper never asked why, he said he was looking for a place to bed down for the night if they had a hotel in Buffalo Ford.

The easygoing Scotchman said, "Och, we've twa hotels but take my word, it's the Box Elder up on yon corner ye want to bye wi'. Tell 'em MacPherson sent ye and they'll treat ye richt!"

Longarm managed not to let it show as he thanked the older man and allowed he'd give the Box Elder a shot. He found the small frame hotel up the block, and it worked like a charm when he told the frosty balding night-clerk MacPherson had sent him.

The night clerk never asked where Longarm had come from, but showed mild concern about his lack of baggage.

Longarm answered easily, "I left my saddle and possibles with other pals here in Buffalo Ford. But I follow your drift and I'll be proud to pay in advance if we ain't talking fancy prices."

45

The clerk said they could let him have a corner room with the cross-ventilation that could get important in August for six bits a night, with the linen changed once a week whether it needed to be or not. So they shook on it, and Longarm registered under his true name without any mention of his federal badge. It was dumb to lie more than one had to.

As he was leaving, the clerk asked who he'd left his saddle with.

Longarm answered on the way out with something that might have been "the Martins." Everybody knew more than one Martin, and it still sounded less made-up than Smith or Jones.

So now he'd established a local residence, should anybody ask, and he'd warned Tess Hayward he might. So she'd suggested he get back in touch with her at her cottage after business hours, or just pay a call on her at her office on Union Square near the municipal corral.

Feeling surer of his bearings, once he'd strode down to the creek and back again, Longarm quietly entered the noisy card house, drifted to the bar, and ordered a schooner of suds to nurse as he lounged there with one boot on the brass rail and the brim of his Stetson shading his tanned face from the coal-oil lamp right above him.

For a long time, nothing happened. If any of the locals noticed him, they didn't seem to give a shit. There were nine games in progress at as many tables under one overhead lamp apiece. The card players seemed the usual mix of cowhands in town for the evening and more sedately dressed gents who could have passed for local businessmen, traveling salesmen, or professional gamblers. This late in the game, few full-time gamblers sported riverboat sombreros, brocaded silk vests, or asked you to call them "Doc." One game in a far corner was being conducted amid fumes of expensive cigars and hilarity. The other games seemed way more serious. Nobody anywhere in

46

the joint wanted to talk to Longarm about Big Dick Wilcox. So he was fixing to mosey out as quietly when there appeared in the doorway a gringo version of a top matador's grand entrance, complete with his parade of *banderilleros*. The big flashy cuss wore a large white cowboy hat, peaked Texas style, and a fringed white buckskin vest over a maroon sateen shirt. His Louis Napoleon mustache and Van Dyke looked as if he'd used boot blacking on them. Longarm knew before the regulars greeted him with a hail of admiration that he was in the presence of Big Dick Wilcox, and the asshole looked as bogus as a three-dollar bill.

Swaggering over to the long bar and bellying up to it with his boys a few yards clear of Longarm, Big Dick declared a round of drinks were on him, and some of the cardplayers actually got up from their games to join the big spender and his quartet of lesser lights.

When the barkeep got around to asking Longarm what his own pleasure might be, Longarm allowed that seeing he wasn't paying for it, he could go for a shot of Maryland rye if they had it.

They did, along with another beer to chase it. Longarm raised the shot glass in a silent toast to the big spender treating them all. But Big Dick didn't seem to notice.

Longarm shrugged, murmured, "Up yours!" and downed the expensive rye, figuring he had enough grub in his gut to handle it.

Big Dick made his stand with his back to the bar and one boot heel hooked over the brass rail, as he rested his elbows on the mahogany to let his hamlike hands dangle over the ivory-gripped and silver-mounted Dance Dragoon conversions riding in matching Slim Jim holsters.

As Big Dick held court, with Longarm just within earshot along the bar, lesser lights came forward as if approaching some manor lord for favors, and the bastard hadn't even been elected yet.

The favors asked were about those you'd expect in a cow town card house frequented by losers. An eavesdropper less experienced in small-town politics than a West-by-God-Virginia boy might have missed Big Dick's motives for what seemed snap judgments about who deserved a hand or who might just be beyond help, no offense.

As each supplicant spelled out his current fix, Big Dick quietly but firmly established where they worked, who they rode for, and how long they might have been around Buffalo Ford Township. The four-flushing cuss was winnowing registered voters from unfortunates he could afford to snub. Anyone could see it cost less to tide a pal over till payday when you turned down transients with a smile. So Big Dick wasn't the total sucker he appeared. Portia and Tess had been right about him. He was brazenly out to buy the election.

But where in the U.S. Consitution did it say a flashy cuss with lots of money couldn't dispense favors in a cow town card house, and what the hell was a totally disgusted lawman supposed to do about a smug outsider out to make himself more welcome when the rascal wasn't breaking any damned old laws?

Longarm knew he didn't even have a good excuse to talk to Big Dick unless he aimed to make up a hard-luck story.

As he nursed his beer and bided his time, Longarm allowed his eyes to drift idly back and forth across the vast smoke-filled interior of the joint. Some few games were still in progress. Some of the players shot dirty looks at Big Dick from time to time. Longarm saw he wasn't the only one in town who found his flashy act distasteful. Longarm's eyes swept over, then back, to fix on a vaguely familiar face in a far corner. Then he looked away before the cuss noticed he was the object of Longarm's interest. Longarm was still wondering who the cuss was, knowing he was almost surely a rider of the owlhoot trail, when a young severely suited gent sporting a pewter badge and a Schofield .45-23 bellied up beside Longarm to remark in a friendly enough but no-bullshit tone, "Howdy, stranger. I'd be Deputy Town Marshal Saul Tanner, and you might be . . . ?"

Longarm said, "Just passing through. Got a room for the night at your Box Elder Hotel up the street."

The town law's voice got ten degrees colder as he pointed out, "I never asked you where you were *at,* stranger. Anyone can see you are at this here bar in my town. I asked you who the fuck you *were,* and I don't mean to ask that half as polite a third time!"

Chapter 6

Longarm tried a high sign familiar to most experienced lawmen and bounty hunters. As he'd feared, Deputy Tanner was not an experienced lawman. He demanded, "Are you mocking me?"

Seeing the fat was in the fire no matter how he answered, Longarm replied, "Nope, but let's keep it down to a roar. I'm riding with you federal. They sent me up to Cheyenne to pick up a famous felon, and I got a tip he was hanging out in this nearby luxury resort."

Longarm was all too aware that Big Dick, down the bar, could hear every word as young Saul Tanner replied in a dubious tone, "Let's see your badge and warrant then. Any saddle tramp or horse thief can *say* he rides for the law!"

Staring thoughfully at that familiar face in the far corner, Longarm said, "Later. Help me with the arrest and I'll be proud to write you up for an assist."

Then he headed through the drifting tobacco smoke without waiting for an answer. Deputy Tanner gulped and dropped his gun hand to the grips of his Schofield to tag along.

Behind them, Big Dick Wilcox quietly snapped, "Truman, Laredo, back their play!" and two of his coterie stepped away from the bar, smiling hard-eyed.

So Longarm found himself leading a modest posse that was still way larger than you needed to bust a paper hanger. But what the hell, as long as nobody there connected his visit to their town-taming D.A.

Freehand Frank McClerich blanched visibly as he spotted four armed men weaving through the tables toward him, and looked as if he was fixing to puke as he locked eyes with Longarm through the thin blue haze.

Then a swarthy hatchet-faced individual Longarm hadn't been looking at suddenly sprang to his feet a table over, and slapped leather as he crabbed sideways for the front entrance, yelling awful things about Longarm's mother!

Longarm naturally went for his own .44-40, but as it cleared leather the Texan called Laredo fired past Longarm's left elbow to nail the old boy over the heart, bounce him off the wall behind him, and spread him like a bear rug, facedown, on the sawdust between the tables!

In the ear-ringing stillness that followed, Deputy Tanner marveled, "Jesus H. Christ! He must have been wanted bad! Who was he, pard?"

Longarm had no idea. So he murmured, "What's in a name? A rose by any other name could interfere with the U.S. Mails."

As he dropped to one tweed-clad knee in the sawdust, he suggested they find out what name the cuss was using that night to play cards by.

The Leadville library card made out to a Reader Brown didn't tell them much. But when he added it up with a livery deposit receipt out of Cornish, Colorado, the dates betrayed a blue streak north for the state line, and so, thinking back to recent editions of the *Denver Post* and *Rocky Mountain News*, Longarm felt safe to declare, "His real handle was Caleb Ferris. He was a bad breed out of the Indian Territory. Shot a man in Boulder who'd offended him by drawing higher cards in an establishment much like this one. So he was only wanted by the State of Colorado till he made it federal by fleeing across a state line."

Rising back to his considerable height, Longarm told young Tanner, "I understand the family of the man he shot in Boulder has posted quite a bounty on this old boy. You can see I never shot him as he resisted arrest by you and these local possemen, if you'd care to take care of the tedious paperwork for this child."

Tanner started to say Laredo hadn't been working for the township and was likely most in line for any bounty.

Then Big Dick Wilcox called out with his elbows still on the bar, "Laredo works for me, and seeing I'm to be your boss as well come this November, you go on and claim the bounty on the son of a bitch, Tanner. You won't get that raise before I win this fall. So you need it more than Laredo. I pay my boys good. Ain't that right, Laredo?"

The lean, mean Texan so addressed grinned like a coyote regarding a fresh-dropped lamb and called back, "Anything you say, Boss!"

So Big Dick called for another round on him, and amid the hilarity that naturally ensued, Deputy Tanner went to fetch some backup and ask their deputy coroner where he wanted the body for now.

Most everyone else agreed their world was well rid of a poor loser who shot winners in card houses. Hardly anybody there had come to lose.

Longarm hung back from the stampede toward the long bar. So the smaller and sneakier-looking Freehand Frank McClerich spoke to Longarm alone as he sidled up, murmuring, "I know what you were thinking, but I honest-to-God got out of Jefferson Barracks last May Day. I got me my federal release papers here, if you'd care to inspect 'em!"

Longarm lied, "I knew that, Freehand Frank. Couldn't you see it was the late Caleb Ferris back yonder I was after?"

The smaller, somewhat older man who'd forged one government bond too many a few years back insisted, "I've gone straight! Honest to God and twice on Sunday! Met up with the woman I've been searching for all my life and we're married up, legal, and making the first honest money I ever made in my hitherto worthless life!"

"Tell me more," Longarm replied, not really giving a shit, but not wanting to join the conversation along the bar before he figured how he might phrase certain replies to inevitable questions.

Freehand Frank said, "I rid the Crow Creek wagon trace up out of Colorado in the rains of the late April greenup. So I was soaked through and trail-weary when I stopped at this homestead down the other side of the ford to offer the lady of the house a dollar if she'd let me and my pony dry out a tad and mayhaps feed us some soda biscuits and hay."

"I take it she took you up on your offer?" Longarm smiled.

The ex-convict chortled, "Did she ever. Her name is Daisy, but I call her my Prairie Rose and that makes her laugh. She's pretty when I get her to laughing. It ain't her fault she hails from a naturally stout family. She marvels at how skinny I stay no matter how she tries to fatten me up, and Lord have mercy, my Prairie Rose bakes layer cakes that ought to put weight on anybody! She bakes 'em with the fresh eggs, butter, and milk she raises, with me helping, for the Cheyenne Social Club and some big hotel over in Cheyenne. She was a widow woman trying to manage her milch cows, pigs, and chickens alone until I rode in this spring to fall in love at first sight and make

54

an honest woman of her. So, no shit now, let me show you my papers here in private. I, ah, fear my Daisy don't know the true facts of my past."

Longarm said he'd take the convicted forger's word he'd paid his debt.

Freehand Frank said, "I never meant to lie to her. Lies just creep up on a man when he's sparking a lady fair. I told her true, that first rainy morn as she was drying me out and stuffing my gut, that I'd just spent six years in Jefferson Barracks. But what was I to say when she said her late husband had served a couple of hitches in the Army too?"

Longarm laughed at the picture, and assured Freehand Frank that until such time as *he* caught anyone in a lie, such secrets were safe with him.

As they bellied up to the bar a couple of bellies clear of Big Dick and his boys, Longarm consulted his pocket watch and observed, "It's after ten, Frank. Ain't you out playing cards a tad late for a happily married-up nester?"

The erstwhile forger explained, "It's my night to howl. My Prairie Rose just druv a buckboard of produce into Cheyenne. She delivers once a week, does some shopping, and then spends the night with former in-laws in town before driving back in the morning with supplies and a renewed interest in yours truly. She knows I come into town to indulge some bad habits whilst the cat's away, and she says she don't mind as long as I don't go near Gopherhole Gloria or Dirty Dolores with her Pussy Poo. That's what she calls my pecker, and she insists she is the one who holds proven title to every inch of the same."

Longarm didn't care who owned another man's organ grinder, and Freehand Frank's remark about his woman staying in town with kin of an earlier man called for no further questions about their vows. So he casually asked to hear more about Gopherhole Gloria and Dirty Dolores, halfway surprised to hear there was an openly operating

55

whorehouse in a town they said Town-Taming Tess had cleaned up four years earlier.

Freehand Frank hesitated, then said, "Well, as long as it's understood I've never been in either of their parlor houses. I have heard you can have it three ways for three dollars, ass-nekked, or old Gopherhole Gloria will let you get a pants-down-and-skirts-up quick one with her Negro gal for four bits. Two bits for the house and two bits for the Negro gal. Dirty Dolores runs a higher-toned establishment."

"So there are *two* whorehouses here in Buffalo Falls?" asked Longarm.

"More like 'six!" Big Dick Wilcox called out, bulling his way along the bar as lesser mortals crawfished out of his path.

Joining Longarm and Freehand Frank, who commenced to act as if the cat had his tongue, the jovial flashy figure, tall as Longarm and a good twenty pounds wider, explained, "Nothing the town can do about that whorehouse row that's mushroomed up recent on the south bank of Crow Creek. Nothing the law they have here in town *right now* can do leastways. Once I'm elected this November, I mean to petition the County Courthouse in Cheyenne to extend the Township of Buffalo Ford another five or six miles south to the Colorado line."

Holding out two Havana claros as he continued, Big Dick pontificated, "Makes for untidy law enforcement when you allow five miles of wagon trace to lie unincorporated for the squatting. As the District Attorney of Greater Buffalo Ford, I'll send all them whores and their pimps back to the wet rocks they crawled out from under, and your name is . . . ?"

Accepting the expensive cigar, seeing somebody figured to smoke it in any case, Longarm tried modestly offering Custis Long.

It didn't work. Big Dick obviously read the newspapers, blast the vivid imagination of some reporters. So he bellowed for all to hear, "Let's have a moment of reverent silence here, gents! You are drinking on me in the presence of the one and original Longarm! The fastest gun in the West since Cockeyed Jack shot Wild Bill in the Number Ten Saloon!"

He let that sink in before he added, "Me and my pal Longarm were just now talking about how we mean to clean things up in these parts as soon as I'm your district attorney!"

Longarm muttered, "Aw, shit," and put the claro in a breast pocket to hand out later to somebody ugly.

Since he was expected to say something more polite, Longarm said he doubted he'd be in town for their election, and asked in an innocent voice if most townships weren't laid out in six-by-six thirty-six-square-mile plat surveys.

Big Dick replied expansively, "You just heard me call it *Greater* Buffalo Ford. Counties are divided into six-by-six-mile townships for openers, just to keep land titles tidy. But where does it say a growing municipality ain't allowed to expand its city limits? Are Chicago or New York confined to thirty-six square miles? How far would you say the east end of London might be from the west end?"

"I stand corrected," replied Longarm dryly. "It hadn't sunk in that Buffalo Ford was as ambitious a project as Chicago, New York, or London Town."

Big Dick didn't seem to find that amusing. He said, "Extending the limits south to the Colorado line will only enclose us a space about the size of Cheyenne itself. No sense getting too big for our britches, and like I said, I'm more interested in *law and order* than population density. Don't matter if you have hundreds of vacant lots in a town as long as you don't have that many *crooks*, see?"

"I'm commencing too," said Longarm, truthfully enough.

Deputy Tanner came back in with two older gents and a pair of kids in bib overalls with a military litter. As the litter bearers moved over to the corpse against the wall with the deputy coroner in charge, Saul Tanner introduced Longarm to his own boss, Town Marshal Brenner.

Brenner had at least ten years and forty pounds on the taller Longarm. His weathered face was pissed under the railroad brim of his black porkpie Stetson as he got right to the point by stating, "You are one rude son of a bitch and I am purely pissed, Deputy Long! Didn't your momma never tell you it's the custom when any lawman rides into a strange town to let the town law know he's *in* town? You could have got your fool head blown off just now, throwing down on that outlaw you just shot without my deputy here knowing who in the fuck you were!"

Longarm let Big Dick say one of his own boys had gunned the wanted murderer, backing the play of young Deputy Tanner, before he explained with a sheepish grin, "I just got into town after dark. You can ask at the Box Elder if I was in town the other side of sundown. I got a room for the night, meaning to pay the usual courtesy call on you in the morning. I was in the process of identifying my fool self to this sharp-eyed deputy of yours when I suddenly spotted Caleb Ferris in the crowd, and the rest you know."

Marshal Brenner snapped, "The hell you say. Who told you we had us a murderer in our midst? Where have you stabled your mount? How did you get here from Cheyenne if you didn't arrive on horseback?"

Making a mental note to assure Tess her town marshal knew his oats, Longarm said, truthfully enough when you studied on it, "I rode up from Denver on a Burlington day tripper and bummed a ride along the wagon trace as far as the outskirts of your town. Like I said, you and most everything in town had closed for the night and . . ."

"Bullshit! My office and our holding cells over on our Union Square stay open round the clock, seven days a week!" Brenner declared, adding in a hurt tone, "You'd have been able to see that from across the damned street, had you given a shit about common courtesy!"

Longarm shrugged and answered, "So what can I say, dear, after I've said I'm sorry?"

"Nothing, you rude bastard!" snapped the town law as he turned on one heel to join the others gathered over the cadaver across the way.

Young Tanner tagged after him. Young Tanner was no fool.

Big Dick Wilcox chuckled indulgently and observed, "I fear you've made yourself an enemy there, Longarm."

Longarm said, "I noticed. But I reckon I'll be all right as long as I don't rob no banks nor saloons in these parts."

Big Dick nodded knowingly and said, "He's on the prod because his job is on the line. Old Brenner means well, I reckon. But he can't seem to get along with others, and I fear I'll have to get rid of him when I take over in November."

Chapter 7

By the time they'd carried off the cadaver, spread fresh sawdust, and had the card games going again, Big Dick and his honor guard had left to hold court somewhere else. The evening was no longer young, but it wasn't dead yet, and Longarm had left his copy of the *Police Gazette* out at Tess Hayward's with his other possible pleasures, including Tess.

Before he could make more new friends, Longarm quietly left the card house to mosey south to Crow Creek some more. He'd satisfied himself earlier, too easily it now seemed, that since Crow Creek formed the southern limits of Buffalo Ford Township, he had no call to concern himself with the widely scattered lamplights winking from, say, a score of spread-out windows strewn to the invisible horizon after dark. But Freehand Frank had intimated action down that way, and Big Dick had said he meant to annex all the way to the Colorado line as soon as he'd horned in on poor old Tess.

Crow Creek wasn't far. So a few moments later, Longarm was lighting a smoke he'd paid for as he stood alone at the crossroads near the crossing they'd named their fool settlement after.

Crow Creek ran mostly west to east along that stretch, intending to swing south into Colorado an hour or so downstream. The wagon trace he and Tess had taken east from Cheyenne, most of their way, ran along the left bank of Crow Creek, or the north side along that particular stretch. The natural buffalo trail they'd turned into a north-south county road crossed the east-west wagon trace and Crow Creek, where the old buffalo trail had crossed the braided creek for no other reason than it's being there. Natural trails laid out by the instincts of grazing critters tended to follow high-dry footing with open downslope views to both sides as they grazed and worried. So there were no sneaky secret bridge foundations a land-grabber might sell to a railroad. Land-grabbers had tried that on other stretches of the High Plains, and the railroads had just laughed, built around them, and left their mushroom towns to wither and weather away.

Prairie streams described as *rivers* could be waded across most times of the year. When they called a body of water a *creek* in those parts, it meant there were times you hardly saw running water at all.

Like Denver's more famous Cherry Creek, Cheyenne's Crow Creek offered a dry-shoe crossing to any agile man, woman, or child who could hop from one sandbar to another in broad daylight.

Broad daylight was the rub. As he stared pensively at what could be made out by the dark of the moon, Longarm decided not to chance a knee-deep surprise or patch of boot-sucking quicksand in the dark.

From where he stood just north of the purling inky crossing, Longarm could make out the row of what he'd taken earlier to be simply town houses on the outskirts of town. If they were what Freehand Frank had called them, they were laid out almost scientifically, along instead of across the route drovers or old boys just out for good times would be following en route to the loading chutes of Cheyenne. Like most such cow towns of the high plains, Buffalo Ford, just out of Cheyenne—like Aurora, just out of Denver, or Elkhorn, just out of Omaha—caught a lot of pocket jingle in addition to their local crossroads trade off dry and dusty riders stopping short of the brighter city lights to make camp, clean up, and often have cheaper rustic fun without big-city prudes calling the durned law on a whippersnapper just acting natural.

The widely scattered windows further from the trail curving over the far horizon into Colorado figured to be homesteads such as that of Freehand Frank and his Prairie Rose, close enough to Cheyenne as well as the more modest Buffalo Ford to run butter, eggs, garden truck, or an occasional side of pork or veal in by buckboard. So assuming the county machine would let a new board of township aldermen annex all that taxable property to the south . . .

"Tess was right!" Longarm brightened, confiding to the inky waters and the ruby tip of his lit cheroot. "Big Dick Wilcox, wherever he went to school, if he ever went to school, never studied municipal law for sour apples!"

Waving his smoke like a baton at the winking lights across the stream, he laughed. "I'm just an old country boy, and *I* can see why the district attorney they already have feels no call to claim another thirty or more square miles of nothing but trouble!"

As pleased with Tess Hayward's legal expertise as no doubt the Wyoming Bar Association, Longarm ambled back up Main Street as far as the first downright noisy old-fashioned raw-lumber saloon. He glanced in to see Big Dick Wilcox and his cronies at the hub of the festivities. Longarm had taken Big Dick's easy measurements already. So he moved on.

He moseyed on up to the wine theater, as one described a fancier saloon offering stage shows against the back wall. He surmised he'd just missed the last show when he

63

spied the small combination of music makers packing up. The asbestos curtain had been lowered for the night, but of course some born night owls were still ordering from scattered tables or bellied along the ornate bar.

At one end of the bar, backed into an angle like a stag at bay, he saw the surly black-hatted Marshal Brenner arguing with other late-nighters. Longarm bellied up a fathom away to listen some before he put an oar in.

As he received his own nightcap, it developed the dispute was between the town law and a town alderman, a know-it-all blacksmith, and one of the town drunks. The three of them seemed put-out about the sheriff's department, over in nearby Cheyenne, grave-robbing the late Calvin Ferris away from them, dad blast it.

Longarm nursed his needled beer as the older lawman tried to explain. "Our fucking deputy coroner by definition works for the fucking county coroner! As soon as they heard about the shooting at the county morgue, they sent a meat wagon out our way for the fucking remains! That's the way the fucking system works!"

Seeing a chance to mend some fences, Longarm sidled closer to nod at the older lawman and proclaim, "Marshal Brenner's right. That's the way things are set up around here."

The alderman asked who the hell Longarm was.

Marshal Brenner introduced them, adding, "I agree he's rude as all get-out, but he likely knows as much as *you* about municipal laws and such, Alderman Redfern!"

Favoring Longarm with a frosty smile, Brenner suggested, "Tell him what county he's in, Longarm."

Longam smiled at the prissy-looking hardware man cum elected petty official and said, "Have a cigar and I'll be proud to spell it out for you."

He politely thumbnailed a light for the claro he'd paid nothing for as he went on. "Wyoming Territory, like New Mexico, Arizona, and other such federal territories, so far, is governed from the territorial capital of Cheyenne by a federally appointed governor and his cabinet. After that, those parts of the territory settled enough to incorporate as counties. This whole southeast corner of Wyoming Territory is now incorporated as the county of Laramie, Cheyenne being the county seat as well as the territorial capital. Are you with me so far?"

Redfern replied defensively he guessed he knew what a county was, seeing he was an elected alderman of one of its fucking townships!

Longarm smiled down at the part-time politico as he relentlessly but not unkindly insisted, "One township among many, each with county deputies appointed by the county board of supervisors in Cheyenne. You get to elect your own mayor, board of aldermen, justice of the peace, and district attorney. They, in turn, appoint the town law, dog catcher, street sweepers, and such."

Marshal Brenner snapped, "Watch who you're mocking, you asshole kid!"

Longarm said soothingly, "Ain't mocking. Telling the way things work. Had I managed to arrest Calvin Ferris on that federal charge earlier, I'd have turned him over to the federal courts in Cheyenne and your U.S. Attorney would have handled the paperwork. Had Ferris shot me instead, it would have been a matter for your county coroner, county sheriff, and county courts. Him getting shot instead by a county resident makes it the business of your county coroner's jury to no doubt decide he had it coming. Your justice of the peace or municipal magistrate just ain't got the clout to handle any offenses punishable by more than, say, thirty days or thirty dollars."

The town drunk stared owlishly and decided, "The hell you say! Ain't you never heard of Justice of the Peace Roy Bean, the only law west of the Pecos?"

Longarm sipped some suds and said, "I have. It's my fervent hope reporters have just made up some of that

65

shit. Old Roy Bean's a saloon keeper and part-time justice of the peace. If he's ever told anybody he presided over a hanging offense, he's been stirring absinthe into his laudanum."

The blacksmith demanded, "What in the hell are we doing with our own District Attorney of Buffalo Ford if she don't have no fucking powers to hang nobody?"

Brenner told him not to talk that way about a lady whether he'd voted for her last time or not.

Longarm said, "No district attorney has the power to hang anybody. Each district or subdivision of a county has its own paid-up-full-time attorney to prosecute anybody arrested by its local law over in one of the *county courts* in the county seat of Cheyenne. Ain't that the way your hear it, Marshal Brenner?"

The older lawman grudgingly growled, "Damned right. You commit a crime in Buffalo Ford Township, me and my boys will bust your ass and Miss Tess Hayward will press charges against you in the county courts or even the terrritorial courts if you don't watch out!"

"There you go," said Longarm, adding, "No offense, gents, but your fair city out this way is little more than an outlying suburb of Cheyenne to the powers that be."

"Then why are we having such a contest over the next district attorney?" demanded Alderman Redfern, as if he'd just noticed he had next to no idea what his mostly honorary position entailed.

He'd answered his own question, in Longarm's view. But seeing the simp had asked, Longarm explained, "Unless you gents run this trail town a lot different from most, you elect a part-time mayor and his board of aldermen for advice and consent. Anyone can see there ain't enough city planning involved to keep your city hall open every day."

"We hold a town meeting to decide when something special needs to be done," objected the alderman, who, now that he studied on it, hadn't been to the past few board meetings.

Longarm nodded, but said, "A town this size nigh runs itself as long as you keep law and order. To make sure of that, you need, and so you have, a full-time if modest police force, a volunteer fire department, and your afore-mentioned district attorney, the only civic official who needs to know one's ass from his or her elbow. Aside from prosecuting local crimes, your paid-up *attorney* ad-vises you all on past or present town ordinances, petitions the court in Cheyenne in your town's behalf, and in sum needs to be a fair lawyer who knows what he or she is doing."

Alderman Redfern demanded, "Then how come she told our mayor it was a bad notion to petition the county for an extension of our city limits as far south as the Colorado line?"

The blacksmith chimed in. "This lazy marshal here could do something about Gopherhole Gloria and Dirty Dolores if we annexed the land all them whores are squat-ting on!"

Longarm snorted, "You mean he could run them south to the Colorado line, and then you'd have thirty or forty square miles of mostly open space you'd be duty-bound to serve and protect."

He let that sink in, and mildly asked, "To what advan-tage to anybody up to anything here in Buffalo Ford?"

The alderman, being a politician, came up with: "For openers, we'd sure be expanding our tax base! All them new residents we'd have to service own *property,* don't they?"

Longarm smiled at Marshal Brenner and asked, "Do you want to tell him, or must I?"

Brenner smiled for the first time since Longarm had seen him and chortled, "Asshole! Property taxes are col-lected by the *county* by the *sheriff's department,* and all that property you want to annex is already *in* Laramie County *being* taxed!"

67

There came a long moment of silence. Then the black-smith asked in a thoughtful tone, "In that case, why does Big Dick yonder mean to annex everything south to the Colorado line?"

Longarm turned, his nightcap half-consumed, to see the snow-white and jet-black figure of Big Dick standing there, not smiling. So Longarm suggested, "Why don't you ask *him*? I ain't the one running for office come November."

Then Big Dick laughed easily and declared, "That's a right smart question and it deserves a straight answer."

So Longarm just waited.

Big Dick saw the others were waiting too. He laughed boyishly and confided, "If you boys repeat a word of this, I'll have to say I never said what I'm about to say."

Longarm just waited as he watched rats run around in the other man's eyes for a spell. Then Big Dick confided, "These lawmen are right. It would be asking for trouble even if we could get the county to extend our township half that far. But none of them whores across the creek *know* that, and just you watch 'em pull up stakes and haul ass as soon as I'm elected and just *petition* the county courts to let us incorporate the open range they're squatting on, see?"

They seemed to. Longarm finished his nightcap and allowed he was up past his bedtime. As he headed for the front entrance, Big Dick fell in at his side to quietly ask, "Why did you just cross me like that, Denver boy? You don't have no dog in this fight, do you?"

"I call 'em as I see 'em," Longarm calmly replied.

Big Dick said, "So I've noticed. As for myself, I've always found it easy enough to make enemies without going out of my way to stomp on toes. So take some fatherly advice in the spirit it's intended and never stomp on my toes again, old son!"

68

Chapter 8

It was darker when he got outside. It appeared they didn't oil the streetlamps to burn all night, and half the saloons had already closed. So as he turned north toward his hotel, Longarm almost missed the forlorn female form seated on a Saratoga trunk near the alley exit to the south till she let out a fervent prayer, or curse, in some lingo that sounded like French with a Scotch brogue.

Turning back to her, Longarm ticked his hat brim to her in such light as there was and said, "Your servant, ma'am. Might you be having some troubles here?"

To which she replied in a lilting but mighty pissed accent, "I am indeed, look you! For I paid those stagehands twenty-five pence apiece, in advance, to carry this trunk back to my hotel, and I fear they took my money and ran off to Gopherhole Gloria's!"

Longarm smiled down at her and said, "In that case they ought to be back soon. But I reckon I can manage that Saratoga if it ain't full of scrap iron. Which hotel might you want it carried to, Miss . . . ?"

"Price-Jones, Glynis Price-Jones, look you, and it's at the Box Elder Hotel I'd be staying," she replied. "But this

69

trunk full of stage costumes and streetwear would be too heavy for one man, you see!"

He suggested, delicately, that she shift her ass off her trunk and give him a shot at it.

He saw she was right as soon as he got a grip on the leather hand straps to tilt it on one end. But he'd made his brag and he was stuck with it. So he took a deep breath, gritted his teeth, and heaved the shitty Saratoga up on one shoulder to commence staggering north without giving it time to drive him shin-deep into Main Street.

The Saratoga trunk was so called because it had been designed with the resort season in Upstate New York in mind. Eastern society gals only wore a fresh gown to dinner for fourteen nights in a row as a rule. So the Saratoga was smaller than a steamer trunk with its top arched sort of like a sea chest. He was having too much trouble breathing to more than grunt back at her as she tagged along, treating him to her not-unfamiliar tale of woe.

He'd known as soon as she'd given her name that she was one of those Welsh gals. It seemed all the gals who'd ever gone on the London stage were Jewish or Welsh. But she *hadn't* been done wrong by a louse who'd lured her out to the American West with false promises, and her show at the wine theater *hadn't* folded to leave her stranded in high summer on the High Plains. She explained she'd agreed to work at their price for the first week, expecting a raise if she brought in a bigger crowd. So she had and they hadn't and she'd just quit, so there.

It was only a million miles up the dark deserted street to the dimly lit entrance to the Box Elder Hotel. So Longarm somehow managed, and as she followed him in, he gasped, "Take the lead and don't ask me to put this down outside your door, ma'am!"

As Glynis nodded and scampered for the stairs, the night clerk, bless his hide, came around the end of his counter to give Longarm a hand.

The two of them still had a time getting the Saratoga up the stairs to the third fucking floor, with its owner leading the way and other guests cracking their doors along the hallway to see what on earth was going on out there.

But at last the heavy trunk was safely on the rug near the window of the Welsh showgal's hired room. That was when they first got a good look at one another, and from the startled smile on her elfin face, she was pleasantly surprised by what she saw too.

You didn't tip hotel help as exalted as room clerks until it came time to settle up and leave. But Glynis held a hand out to the old night clerk as she thanked him in that lilting accent, and Longarm half-expected the cow-town cuss to kiss it before he backed out, blushing like a fool kid. Longarm believed what she'd said about drawing a good crowd to that wine bar.

She stood about five-one in her French heels, and despite her proper summer frock of beige shantung, you could see she was built like a wasp.

No natural woman had ever been created with curves like those, but if her heroically cinched whalebone stays hurt her that tight, she bore up well under pain. Longarm knew, because he'd asked a library gal, that the witches and fairies in children's books illustrated in England had been modeled on the natural features of Welsh country gals and the Sunday-go-to-meeting costumes of prosperous Welsh wives, pointy hats and all.

Aside from her heart-shaped elfin face, Glynis Price-Jones had red hair and chocolate eyes a man sure felt like drowning in, even after a day in the sack with the local district attorney.

So it was likely thanks to Town-Taming Tess that as soon as Glynis told him she'd arranged to have her pretty self and her heavy baggage driven over to Cheyennc the next day, he was able to say without pain that in that case they'd best say good night.

When she graciously held her hand out to him, Longarm gave in to his impish impulse to raise it to meet his lips like she was a countess or something.

It didn't fluster her. She dimpled up at him and told him that it had tickled, and added, "You've yet to tell me your own name, Sir Galahad, if I'm not mistaken?"

He let go of her hand with a laugh and replied, "My poor but honest parents named me Custis. Custis Long. But I reckon you're used to bringing out the Sir Galahads in all of us, Miss Glynis."

She frowned and said, "I'll have you know I really paid those stagehands who betrayed my trust, look you! I'll not have you thinking I'd be one of those satin teases who boo-hoo-hoo favors out of gentlemen!"

Longarm assured her calling him a gentleman was more than enough, and got the hell out of there before he could get in more trouble.

Back in his own room, as he hung his .44-40 handy on a bedpost and shucked to turn in bare-ass, Longarm shook his head in wonder as he felt those familiar stirrings in his naked loins. For the gal had just *said* she was leaving town in the morning, and had she stayed on at the wine theater, what sort of a skirt-chasing twit would make a play for another gal in the same town as Town-Taming Tess?

Trimming the lamp and sliding his bare hide between clean cotton sheets, he considered how old Tess, out at her cottage, was likely as lonesome in bed as he was just then, if she was still awake. He'd warned her he might stay in town if that worked to their advantage. But she'd likely waited up past her usual bedtime, and damn it to hell, it was time to get some sleep, not a time to picture naked ladies alone in other beds!

But as in that Russian folk tale calling for a kid to sit

in the woods after dark and not think one time about *bears,* trying not to think about a buxom towheaded town tamer or an elfin redheaded showgal alone in bed on the same planet was like trying not to think about someday dying, how long was forever, or how high was *up,* as your mind got to wandering the wonderlands between awake and asleep.

"You could have at least *tried,* seeing she'll be out of town long before Tess might ever notice she passed through!" his glans complained to his brain.

Longarm growled, "Hold the thought for the next time we find our fool selves alone with Tess and don't be so damned sure of yourselves! You mind that time in the shay out to Cherry Hill?"

His mortified glans didn't answer. His brain had forgiven them for their unexpected failure to rise to the occasion after all that trouble getting that giggling schoolmarm out to that lovers' lane on the rolling prairie east of Denver. Longarm was still working on whether his glans had acted out of some sixth sense, or just because he'd been in bed with those bawdy roommates the night before. But in the end he'd been glad he'd had to graciously give in to her protestations of virginity and drive her home as pure as he'd found her. For he'd only found out later she was married to a railroad man who'd left her with a little extra bedtime in her lap.

Consoling himself with the notion Glynis Price-Jones was likely a gold digger and possibly potbellied when she took that corset off, Longarm spent some time wondering whether those canals the professors had just noticed on Mars might be real, and how anybody was ever going to find out, and then the next thing he knew two teamsters seemed to be calling each other cocksuckers down on Main Street, and when Longarm opened his eyes, the bright morning sun was poking holes in his window blinds. So he muttered, "Must be six at the earliest!" and got up.

73

Once he'd treated himself to a whore bath at the corner washstand and hauled his duds on, Longarm found a stand-up beanery near his hotel and stoked his furnace with bacon and biscuits, hot tamales and black coffee.

By this time, Buffalo Ford was waking up and making more sense as to why it was there. In a world literally running on horsepower, a trail town every hour or so along a busy trail suited the fancies if not the needs of traffic on the hoof. Longarm could see from the hours the shops along Main Street kept that Buffalo Ford served the needs of the farmers and stockmen this far out of Cheyenne as well. They weren't doing much trade on a weekday morn at the Methodist church he passed as he ankled on over to Union Square to pay that formal courtesy call he owed the town law's desk log and ask if he'd missed anything after turning in so early.

Union Square was situated sensibly upwind of the municipal corral and the now-busy as well as dusty Main Street. As he strode across the tawny close-cropped and summerkilt grass, he admired the brass twelve-pounder defending the center of the square with its plugged muzzle pointed ever southeast toward the heart of the Confederacy, and he saw they'd planted some cottonwood saplings that promised some shade in mayhaps another dozen years. The saplings looked to be about four years old. He nodded and murmured, "Nice touch, Tess."

Over to the northwest, facing the square with its back to the wolf winds of a Wyoming winter and the glare of its summer afternoon sun, a barn-sized meeting hall dominated lesser white-frame buildings trying to look official with their Federal moldings and pillars of the stern Doric Order, made out of wood but covered with more than one coat of high-priced lead paint.

When he introduced himself to the deputy in his teens holding down the desk out front of their patent cells, Longarm was told Marshal Brenner usually showed up

74

around nine unless he heard gunshots or something.

Longarm signed their log book and offered the squirt a smoke he'd paid for as he established with casual questions that Hizzoner, their part-time mayor, was on tap if need be at his cattle spread just past the outskirts of town. For as Longarm had already assumed, most of the *easy* elected positions in the township were held by local bigwigs who enjoyed the titles and not being bossed by the same, as long as they didn't have to *do* a whole lot.

Like their female district attorney, they had a full-time justice of the peace working out of his own house up the wagon trace a piece. Longarm knew, as he'd explained the night before to Big Dick's displeasure, a small-town J.P. dealt mostly in handing out licenses to run a business, keep a dog, or marry up. He sometimes played old King Solomon in local business or land-title disputes if both sides agreed to the notion. Serious court cases were heard over in Cheyenne, the town law bearing witness and their pretty D.A. prosecuting the son of a bitch. Their resident undersheriff, postmaster, deputy coroner, and such were all appointed from higher up the chain of command. So with one possible exception, the position of district attorney packed more clout than others below the county level.

Longarm didn't ask the squirt who the secretary treasurer of Buffalo Ford Township might be. He knew it would be listed in their directory, and he wanted to see what sort of library they had in any case. So he thanked the squirt and strode on out into the morning sunlight.

He'd barely gotten his bearings back when a familiar voice trilled his name, and he glanced that way to see Tess Hayward had just reined in on the far side of the meeting hall. So he doffed his hat to her and legged it over to take the ribbons and tether her mule to the cast-iron hitching post in front of a smaller building described as their municipal office building by the gilt wood letters over the Doric capitals framing the door.

As he helped her down, Tess glanced around as if to make sure it was safe to say, "I stored your saddle and Winchester in my cottage. I feared you'd met another woman in town until I got word of that shootout in the card house. Where did you go from there?"

He said, "Thought it best to get a room in the Box Elder. So far, Lord willing and the creeks don't rise, nobody here in town knows we've ever met before. So howdy, and do you mean to leave this pure mule out in the sun like this?"

She said, "I'll have one of my office boys carry it on to the livery stables across the municipal corral. They take good care of us there. Let's get ourselves inside, speaking of hot suns!"

Longarm followed her inside and down a corridor, where a squirt who reminded him of old Henry back in Denver sat playing another typewriter in her front office.

Tess introduced Longarm as a lawman looking into the recent doings of the late Caleb Ferris in their township, asked the squirt to see to her mule, and added they didn't want to be disturbed.

As soon as she had Longarm alone in her back office, Tess shut and barred the door, moaning, "Oh, Lordy, I know I should show some sense and I know someone might come calling any minute, but if we keep most of our clothes on and . . . Help me clear this fucking desk and fuck me, you fool!"

So in the end, Longarm was just as glad he hadn't given in to his own warm nature at his hotel the night before. He'd have never gotten it up again that hard, that soon, had Glynis Price-Jones been half as warm and wet inside.

Chapter 9

That office boy was back on his typewriter out front when Longarm left half an hour later, poker-faced and steady enough on his feet by then, he hoped.

If the squirt suspected anything, he was a good poker player as well. It wouldn't have been polite to ask if her office boy had any notions as to how often Town-Taming Tess had a quickie atop that desk. It was tough to decide whether she'd been bracing her palms against the nearby filing cabinet like so from prior experience or sudden inspiration. He'd never had anyone atop that desk, and he'd still found good handholds to either side of her upward thrusts.

He hadn't asked Tess who their secretary treasurer was because to begin with, it was hard to hold her to such sensible conversation for long, and also because he wasn't sure he trusted her completely.

Legging it across the stubble of Union Square, he fished out a smoke as that small voice of sanity that comes over a man right after a warm meal or a good piece of ass asked, "Are we studying Tess and her ways as we promised Miss Portia, or as a jealous moon calf? Where in the U.S. Constitution does it say we get to play Don Juan and call ourselves a sporting gent if gals can't enjoy the hobbies of Lady Hamilton, and say, wasn't that frisky Miss Nell Gwynn a showgal of the Welsh persuasion?"

In restored humor, Longarm ambled on to their lending library north of the square, and as his eyes adjusted to the light inside, he saw it was just as well he'd just shot his wad standing up. For it allowed a pleasantly surprised man to smile politely down at the gal behind their library desk without grinning like a shit-eating dog with a hardon as he politely asked, "Might you have a township directory on hand here, ma'am?"

She was too young-looking to call ma'am. So he figured she'd like to be treated as respectfully as her grownup job might call for.

She was barely legal, with blond hair two shades darker than the hair he'd just been parting with his old organ grinder. She had big blue eyes that smiled back in a sisterly manner as she produced the modest paper-bound volume he'd requested and asked if he had a library card.

Longarm explained, "I don't need to check no books out, ma'am. I ain't a resident of your fair city. I'm a lawman passing through and I only need a peek at some of your entries, see?"

She did. She stared owl-eyed and gasped, "You're him! That famous Longarm who shot it out with that killer in the card house last night!"

Longarm just muttered, "Aw, mush," as he got out his notebook and a stub pencil to record the few local officials he was serious about, along with their current addresses. He didn't have time to explain all that shit at the card house to begin with, and it wouldn't have made a whole lot of difference if he had. He'd seen that adoring look before. Reporter Crawford of the *Post* grinned at him that way every time a poor working deputy granted the silly bastard an interview. Longarm had given up trying to convince folks with such romantic views of his job that he couldn't really walk on water, or that even Buffalo Bill had been known to miss more than one shot out of every hundred.

He thanked the pretty little thing and put his notes away. She said she was Sue Ellen Garth and she took an hour off for dinner and got off for the evening at sundown.

He soberly thanked her for the information and left. She hadn't had to tell him she still lived at home. A gal that young would never be staying open that late without her parents' permission, and while being a sporting gent was one thing, acting like a total asshole with a home girl was another.

The local position of secretary treasurer for the board of aldermen, presiding over town meetings and on occasion directing their full-time officials to do something unusual, was held by one Herbert Kraft, the manager of their local branch of the Drover's Savings and Loan. It was easy to see why the elected board had appointed him. As in the case of it being a good idea to have a trained lawyer as district attorney, it seemed sensible to have a man who managed money as his trade keep the books and deal with the expenses of their township.

Longarm found the Buffalo Ford branch of Drover's Savings and Loan open for business on Main Street, not far from his hotel. When he asked a teller inside, he was shown back to the office of the portly white-haired branch manager, who had a firm handshake to go with his honest face.

Longarm had yet to meet a banker who *looked* like a crook.

Kraft sat Longarm in a fancier leather armchair than the one in Billy Vail's office, and offered him another free cigar as he allowed he'd been expecting Longarm's visit.

Longarm bought some thinking time by biting off the

tip of the American-made but expensive cigar and lighting up before he asked how come. He wasn't supposed to be in town in connection with the coming elections. But asking a gent how come he'd been expecting you sounded less suspicious than *not* asking him. So Longarm did.

The white-haired banker leaned back expansively with a wave of his own cigar to reply, "You naturally assumed, as we did the moment we heard of him being in town, that that wanted outlaw, Caleb Whatsisname, may have been planning some skullduggery up our way and, well, this *is* the only bank in town!"

Longarm got his own cigar going before he confessed with a sheepish grin a man had to get up early to pussyfoot about money with a banker.

He said, "Frank and Jesse seem to prefer outlying branch banks to hit since they made that awful mistake with that main branch up in Northfield back in '76. Let's talk about how much you might have on hand out this way at a given time. I understand you keep the books and handle the finances for Buffalo Ford Township?"

The banker who did nodded, but answered easily, "Not that much of it lies in our own vaults for any length of time. You're so right about owlhoot riders hitting small-town branch banks with monotonous regularity!"

Kraft smiled a mite smugly and confided, "We barely keep petty cash to pay off day labor for the township here at this branch. I maintain an interest-bearing municipal fund at our main branch over in the capital and county seat. I *try* not to have much of anybody else's cash on hand here at this branch. I draw on our main branch as need be to cover checks and the usual monthly withdrawals of our regular customers."

He looked pained and added, "I must say that free-spending Richard Wilcox, they call him Big Dick, has been messing us up of late and, well, we have had to keep more on hand than usual. But I've asked him to let me fix him up with a checking account drawing on our Cheyenne vaults, and asked some of the merchants here in town to back me up on that if he wants them to vote for him come November!"

"He's been balking at the notion?" asked Longarm casually.

The white-haired older man flushed and said, "He told me to go fuck myself the first time I asked. Said he only hands out checks to the really desperate and deserving, and demanded to know how anybody at all desperate was supposed to cash a check in Cheyenne when they had the wolf at their door here in Buffalo Ford!"

Seeing he had the ball in that court without the banker balking at his line of questions, Longarm blew a thoughtful smoke ring and said, "Heard tell about Big Dick's generous ways. I reckon it must be, ah, privileged information should anybody ask how much the new boy in town might have you holding for him?"

Kraft shrugged and said, "I wish I knew where he keeps his main grubstake! He deposits a thousand-dollar check drawn on our Cheyenne bank once a month to cover the paper he doles out here in the township. As you suggested, I'm not at liberty to reveal the line of credit he has with Drover's Savings and Loan. Suffice it to say it's enough, and they say he maintains his balance in Cheyenne with letters of credit drawn on more than one bigger bank in other parts."

Longarm nodded knowingly and said, "In sum, he's working with a lot of money, possibly for someone else. What's all this I hear about such a free spender running for some office here in town come November?"

Kraft said, "District attorney. He's made no secret about that, and speaking as an unpaid volunteer who's had to work with the asshole aldermen of this wide spot in the trail, he's sure to win!"

Studying the tip of his own cigar, Kraft continued half

to himself, "I mean to resign if he does, of course. Bad enough to work for free for cowboys playing politician and a mayor with a herd to manage, a wife that fools around, and a drinking problem. But I'll be sorry to see Tess Hayward go. I know she's just a gal, but she knows her oats and she and Marshal Brenner have done a fine job here in Buffalo Falls. Old Warren Brenner has declared *he* means to pack it in if they elect that Texas four-flusher too. Says the new D.A. can give his badge to any street sweeper who wants it. But of course one of his kid deputies will probably fill his boots. Or try to. It's a crying shame, but that's what you get when you let even *women* vote, for crying out loud!"

"Big Dick's been buying flowers, books, and candy for the ladies of Buffalo Ford?" asked Longarm.

The banker said, "Worse. He's been buying groceries and paying medical bills for poor but popular old drabs."

Kraft puffed his cigar and almost spat, "After that, Wilcox has been promising them the moon on a fine silver chain of wishing stars! He's promised the W.C.T.U. he'll make the saloons close early on payday, and served notice he means to run those whores down by the creek clean out of Wyoming. Ain't it a bitch how women believe most any promise as long as it's a promise they've been wanting to hear?"

"You don't think he can tame your town better than Miss Tess?" the man who'd just come in their D.A. asked.

Kraft shook his head and said, "Buffalo Ford is already tame as you want any cow town. Miss Tess and Marshal Brenner have done as good a job as anybody could, if not a tad too good for some of our wilder residents. You can only tame a town to where folk still want to live in it. Under Miss Tess and Marshal Brenner, it's understood them whores don't even shop on our side of the creek, the house games are run as the odds are posted, and nothing stronger than liquor is served without prescription at any of the saloons."

Longarm allowed that sounded fair to him. They shook on it and parted friendly. Longarm had long since learned the hard way that most folks spread lies through the most innocent conversations the way a baker tosses raisins into raisin cake, more to sweeten the results than out of evil intent. But he figured Kraft had been lying no more than your average banker, and Longarm saw no way Tess or any other D.A. could get at the operating funds of Buffalo Ford Township.

He made a mental note as he headed back to the Box Elder to see if there were any messages for him yet, to try to learn just how much there might be in the kitty for anybody to try for.

As he'd explained in the wine theater the night before, a township had limited powers of extortion. With the county collecting property taxes, Hizzoner and his part-time aldermen could only collect municipal fees such as licenses to set up shop, fines for falling down drunk in public, and so forth. But all the shit that went on in thirty-six square miles could add up, and so who was he supposed to check with next?

Still studying on that, Longarm returned to the Box Elder to ask at the desk if anybody had left any telegrams or mash notes in his key box. Nobody had. He muttered, "Shit," and turned away to consider where he might enjoy a noon dinner sitting down, for Pete's sake.

That was when he spied Glynis Price-Jones perched on her Saratoga again, under a potted lobby palm with paper leaves. As their eyes met, she smiled gamely. But her chocolate eyes were red-rimmed from hard rubbing. So he ambled over, ticked his hat brim to her, and asked what might be eating her this time.

She confessed, "I've been played for a greenhorn from Welsh Wales again, look you! I see now how the manager of that wine theater has been stringing me along all this while, bless him! One of those very stagehands I told you about last night got another dollar off me this very morning to hire a rig and drive me into Cheyenne, you see! But that was so long ago, and now it's nearly noon and what am I to do when I'm supposed to leave my room at noon?"

Longarm said, "Just set there whilst I amble over to the livery by the municipal corral and see about hiring us a horse and buggy. I was considering a run into Cheyenne this afternoon in any case. I'll be proud to run you and your baggage in, Miss Glynis."

She brightened, clapped her hands, and jumped up to kiss his cheek, standing on tiptoe to do so before she volunteered, "You have to let me pay half, look you! I told you I wasn't one of those boo-hoo-hoos who expect men to pay their way for them!"

He said he'd argue about it on the way to Cheyenne, and sat her back down.

It seemed to the worried Welsh girl that her Sir Galahad was taking his time coming back if all he had in mind was a buggy ride to the county seat. But he was forgiven when he returned with a brown paper sack to say, "Hold on to this load whilst I see about shifting that infernal Saratoga out to the team and surrey I just hired, Miss Glynis. I aim to get us into Cheyenne before the banks close for the day, and it's twenty to twelve here already!"

As he hefted the load and staggered outside with it, Glynis peeked into the brown paper bag to demand, "What on earth are we going to do with these loaves of bread, bottles of beer, and, let's see, cheddar cheese and sliced ham?"

Heaving her trunk into the back of the surrey, Longarm took the bag, deposited it between the sprung seat and dashboard, and helped Glynis aboard as he replied, "Figured we'd save time eating on the fly. They tell me at the

84

livery these matched bays are steady trotters. We'll soon find out. Hang on whilst I untether 'em!"

That took less time than it might to tell about it, and the Welsh gal was laughing fit to bust as they lit out for Cheyenne at a spanky trot. When he asked her what she'd just yelled out in Welsh, she laughed some more and said, "If I wanted you to know, I'd have yelled it in the English, look you!"

Chapter 10

As they trotted past Tess Hayward's cottage, Longarm was just as glad she was in town tending to business after her morning quickie. Glynis was laughing about "wilderness and thou" as she built them heroic ham-and-cheese-on-rye sandwiches. Longarm had read that poem by the romantic Persian poet, so he grinned up the trail ahead and chuckled back:

A loaf of bread beneath the bough.
A book of verse, a loaf of bread, and thou, beside me,
Singing in the wilderness.

Then he dryly added, "I didn't think much of the York State vintage they had in that store."

She allowed beer would do just fine. So they rode along washing down their sandwiches with bottled lager, and after they'd about demolished the bread, Glynis took to singing in the wilderness.

She had a downright good voice, and he believed her when she said that was what she mostly did on stage, along with some shimmy-shaking, and protestations against Queen Victoria's rule that delighted Irishmen as much as or more than her own Taffies, as she described Welshmen.

Longarm dryly observed he'd never agreed with some of Queen Victoria's positions on other matters, confessing he had no idea what Her Majesty was up to in Welsh Wales.

The Welsh redhead didn't seem to be listening as, maybe inspired by bottled lager as much as their invigorating pace, she threw back her pretty red head to howl, to the tune of "Men of Harrow":

Saxons crossed the English channel,
All dressed up in tin and flannel,
Our lads met the foe at Prannel,
Wearing nought but woad!

Longarm didn't grin until it sank in that woad was the blue war paint the ancient Celts had worn while fighting bare-ass. He had to allow she was painting a funny picture as she sang on:

Druid clothes are crafty!
Perhaps a wee bit drafty!
Paint your vest and knickers on,
Don't bother with the seams!

Longarm whipped the rumps ahead of them with the ribbons to get the team in time with her as she wound up:

Saxons suffered plagues and itches,
Running round in wet wool britches!
Our lads fought like sons of bitches!
Wearing nought but woad!

Then she stopped as suddenly as she'd begun to ask in a little-girl voice, "Who are we going to play with in Cheyenne, Daddy?"

Longarm said, "I don't know about you. I want to talk to some bankers about big spenders. At the rate we're rolling, it's still likely to make for a tight fit. So do you mind if I drop you off wherever you want me to after I just might make it to Drover's Savings and Loan on Central Avenue?"

She assured him that since he'd helped her escape the clutches of Buffalo Ford, she had time to burn in Cheyenne. She explained how she'd wired booking agents in San Francisco and New York that she was at liberty and awaiting the best offer at the Mountain Vista on 16th Street near Cheyenne's Union Pacific Depot. When he said in that case he'd be proud to drop her off there after they'd been by the bank to the north, she naturally wanted to know why they were on their way to said bank.

It killed a good stretch of their run to bring Glynis up to date on the tribulations of Town-Taming Tess.

He felt it uncalled for to mention screwing the district attorney of Buffalo Ford. He might have forgotten to tell her they were talking about another woman if Glynis hadn't brightened and said, "Oh, I heard about them electing a woman to that position back in Buffalo Ford, and wasn't that gallant of them, look you! Despite having sat the throne since '37 in skirts, that old bawd Victoria puts even *English* girls in prison when they register to vote, you see!"

So Longarm told her in a more relaxed tone about Big Dick Wilcox horning in far from his Texas roots with lots of money. Being a foreigner, the Welsh gal didn't find it as unusual for a Texas showoff to run for public office in Wyoming.

Not taking time to elaborate on the War Between the

89

States, Longarm said, "Wyoming Territory was part of the Dakota Territory and mostly occupied by Indians during all that feuding and fussing farther east, with some skirmishing as far west as New Mexico. But most of the folk who pioneered Wyoming Territory as Mister Lo, the Poor Indian, and his buffalo were shot off were from Colorado or the Union states of the Middle West. A heap of hard feelings that writers such as Ned Buntline put down to a natural Western wildness are left over from the war."

She nodded and said, "Like the bitterness still festering between my Taffies and the dreadful Brum, it seems. We call the worst of all the English the Brum because they call their den of evil Birmingham, look you!"

He allowed that that seemed about the size of it, but added, "A lot of Wyoming stockmen did drive their seed herds up the Goodnight-Loving Trail from West Texas as the Reconstruction ran down in more recent times. So you do get scattered feuds across the West these days with unreconstructed Rebel cattlemen on one side and the mostly Union business interests in and about your county seats. But Big Dick Wilcox and his money would make more sense bucking for *county* office as he courted the cattle interests for blocks of votes."

She suggested, "Maybe his fellow Texas cowboys don't like him, do you think?"

Longarm said, "I do. Miss Tess Hayward has the Wyoming Stock Growers Association and the Grange backing her bid for re-election. As far I've managed to find out, none of the upright established interests up this way want the flashy four-flusher to replace her. I'm trying to find out who's really grubstaking his brazen attempt at a takeover."

Glynis asked, "What if he's simply a rich eccentric?"

Longarm shook his head and said, "He ain't spending his own money. He's too free and easy with money to be spending his own. I've met genuinely generous rich folk.

They like to see good value for their charity. Big Dick Wilcox throws money around with the wicked grin of a mean little kid busting windows. I doubt he's paying for the rocks!"

"Then you suspect he's fronting for *really* mean rich kids who want him to . . . what?" she asked with a puzzled frown.

He said that once he'd guessed that, he'd know who, and what might be done about them. So she suggested they get it on over to that bank.

They had to stop halfway in a cottonwood grove to rest the team in some shade while Glynis went for a walk in the woods to powder her nose, she said. Longarm pissed on the other side of the surrey before he broke out the nose bags, made his way down the steep clay banks of Crow Creek, and half-filled them with creek water and handfuls of cottonwood leaves. Cottonwood being a breed of poplar, such fodder set well in horseflesh.

As they drove on, they spied the peaks of the Laramie Range ever closer as they topped each rise. Like Denver almost due south, Cheyenne spread out across the rolling prairie aprons of mountains that looked a lot closer than they really were, the Laramies being a tad lower than the Front Range looming west of Denver.

Knowing his way around Cheyenne, Longarm knew better than to follow the creek-side route far as Logan Avenue before swinging north away from Crow Creek and across the U.P. right of way east of the sprawl of yards. He circled west past the glorified prairie bog they'd taken to calling Lake Minnehaha, for Gawd's sake, and through the fashionable Rainsford district, where some street trees were getting tall enough to cast some shade and they swept up the horseshit regularly.

Central Avenue, as its name indicated, ran north through the center of town from just east of the Union Pacific Depot, or "Uncle Pete's" as it was locally known.

Cheyenne owed its location to nearby Fort Russell, built to keep tabs on the Tsitsissah or Sha-hi'yenah, and "The Gangplank," as they called a straight and gentle pass through the otherwise rough and rocky Laramie Range to the west. The combination of a railroad leap from the High Plains over the Shining Mountains and a strong Army base to keep the Crooked Lancers away from the mostly Irish track layers, that far east, had resulted in a railroad-military-cattle center that couldn't have avoided growing into a city had it wanted to.

Longarm was still working on what Big Dick and his hidden backers were trying to grow just over the horizon to the east as he reined in before Drover's Savings and Loan and suggested Glynis tag along and get out of the afternoon sun.

She seemed to feel that was a grand notion, and gave him a hug as he helped her down. He tethered the team and they moseyed on in.

They'd made it to Cheyenne better than half an hour before closing time. But the son-of-a-bitching branch manager had left early for the day and try as he might, Longarm couldn't get a single soul in the infernal bank to even admit they *had* a client called Wilcox.

When a priss who looked the way Henry back in Denver might wind up in his fifties, if he didn't watch out, suggested Longarm come back in the morning, Longarm said, "I aim to, with a court order to examine your books if this puffed-up Mr. Harrison of yours doesn't make my next visit worthwhile, and you can tell him I said so!"

Glynis Price-Jones didn't seem half as upset at the thought of his being stuck in town overnight. When they got back outside and he circled the block to head down Capitol Avenue for her hotel, Glynis suggested he might care to stay there overnight as well, seeing the hotel had its own stable and stood so handy to his bank.

He declared it wasn't his bank, and didn't go into the

simple fact he was on his own time and couldn't charge fancy hotel rates to his field expenses, blast all bankers and the hours they chose to keep.

By the time they got to the Mountain Vista, he'd decided the six bits or so he'd save on a cheaper room weren't worth the awkwardness, once Glynis had coyly suggested he have supper on her to pay him back for such an amusing ride into town.

When they got there, a pair of stalwart bellboys were proud to take her Saratoga and her carpetbags upstairs for her, once she'd registered and found, sure enough, two Western Union telegrams had been awaiting her arrival. Longarm bet another bellboy four bits he couldn't see to the hired team and surrey for him. He lost, and followed the gal and her baggage upstairs as she tore open the telegrams to read on the fly. She was smiling sort of wistfully as she tipped the help and saw them out. As she turned back with a sigh, Longarm asked if she'd been sent bad news by wire.

She waved him to a seat on a satin love seat, any beds in her three-room suite being off the cozy sitting room, and sat down beside him to unpin her red hair as she said, "I don't feel like going out to supper after that long drive. Why don't we have them send up their menu?"

He said, "It's early to be that serious about supper, Miss Glynis. I take it both them telegrams are Welsh state secrets?"

She sighed again and said, "Alas, my cup runneth over. I seem to have my choice of seacoasts, New York and San Francisco both having oodles of Irishmen who despise Queen Victoria more than I do!"

"Well, that's great. Quitting that wine theater hasn't left you in a fix after all." Longarm smiled.

She replied, "I just said that. Both booking agents expect a reply in the near future. No matter which I choose, it means we only have this one night to . . . remember."

Longarm asked her permission to smoke, grabbing for something more innocent to do with his hands than his hands wanted him to let them do.

She said it would be all right if they could have the windows open.

He said, "You're right, they're a pungent brand and I smoke too much out on the range."

"You're evading my question, Custis," she softly trilled.

He nodded and said, "I know. I ain't used to discussing such topics with such . . . sophisticated ladies."

She laughed, a shade bitterly, and asked, "What do you take me for, a perishing Right Honorable because of my British accent? Do you know how I was greeted by a stuck-up English actress the first time I met her?"

She struck a pose and recited mockingly.

Taffy was a Welshman,
So Taffy was a thief!
Taffy came to our house,
And stole a side of beef!

He nodded soberly and said, "If it's any comfort, such snobs look down on pure Anglo Saxons who didn't go to the same fancy schools with 'em. I've often wished I was a member of some despised race so's I could say that was how come they were mocking me. But leaving our accents aside, Miss Glynis, if you got to head east or west on the double and I have to head back to Buffalo Ford in the morning . . ."

She cut in. "We'll only have one night and such daylight as we still have to play games in."

She struck another pose, her spine arched and her hip touching Longarm's thigh, and laughed. "Try this for sophisticated British humor. It was on a powder room wall in Mayfair."

94

There was a young blade named Skinner,
Who took a young lady to dinner,
At quarter to nine they started to dine,
At quarter past ten it was in her.
Not skinner,
The dinner,
Skinner was in her before dinner!

So Longarm laughed, as any young blade might have, took her in his arms, and damned if he wasn't in her before dinner!

Chapter 11

"Dinner" was what folks who ate it in London Town called supper. They called a regular dinner *lunch*. Once Glynis and Longarm were going at it right in the adjoining bedroom, he saw he'd been right about that wasp waist. Glynis said all that whalebone encased in black satin and lace felt fine where it was when he suggested unlacing it for her dog-style. So he just had to put up with that fourteen-inch waist dividing heroic breastworks and considerable bare ass for such a bitty gal, although he suspected that as Glynis likely knew, all that whalebone added to the voluminous top and bottom since her true waist measurement had to go *some* damned where.

The impulsive showgal naturally had a modest kimono stored away in that Saratoga, so when he'd pounded her to glory more than once and she got over crying about nothing that was worth a shit everlasting, she yanked the bellpull by the bedboard, put the kimono on, and went out to the hall door, where, sure enough, a bellboy showed up within minutes to take her order for an intimate dinner for two.

That was what she called filet mignon with mashed potatoes and French-cut string beans, dinner for two.

97

They ate it bare-ass in bed with the tray between them so they could admire the sunset out the window. The orange and purple sky outlining the jaggedy black-paper silhouette of the Laramies got her to sobbing again. He knew better than to ask why. But Glynis softly explained with less sass in her lilting voice, "The first time I took the Channel steamer to Calais, I fell in with a band of young Scots, on holiday for some Caledonian occasion. They'd naturally brought two pipers along, and after I'd taught one lassy to wish death on the English in Welsh instead of her Gaelic, I was joyfully included in their party."

She sighed wistfully and continued. "The poor Channel-crossing Lime Juicers on board moved forward as we ruled the stern, pipes skirling, ale and porter flowing, and skirts kilted high as we tripped the light fantastic to make the heaving deck drum so hard, a crewman came aft to make sure we weren't steaming through the night with a bent screw."

Longarm said, "Sounds like fun. I've been to a few parties like that."

Glynis sighed. "*Few,* all too few, is the fly in the ointment of our mayfly lives! That one magic night ended in a way I don't think I ought to tell a lover, and I confess I was looking forward to the crossing when it came time to return from the Continent. But there was no magic to be found. Nobody else on board seemed interested in anything but reading in a deck chair or heaving up over the side, look you! I do believe I've been to the Continent six times in all, adding up to a dozen crossings, and save for that one magic time, they've all been endlessly dull!"

Longarm tried some French-cut string beans. They weren't bad if you liked rabbit food. He washed his mouth out with their fancy chickory-tainted coffee and said, "I know this Denver society gal who will plan fancy get-togethers with her help serving whore's ovaries made with all sorts of expensive funny-tasting stuff, and she was always complaining that no matter how she tried, she could never get her whore's ovaries to taste as good as some she'd had back East as a college gal."

"Was she as good in bed as me?" Glynis pouted.

Longarm said, "We were talking about *unexpected* pleasures. Nobody ever expects slap-and-tickle to be unpleasant. My point is that one evening when she'd dragooned me into taking her to the infernal opera, the fancy restaurants all around, catering to the after-the-show folk, were all jam-packed. So, rather than stand with her like hogs pent in a red velvet sty, I hauled her over to this Mex joint I knew near the stockyards, and do you know that for all her fancy education and fancy whore's ovaries, that poor gal had never tasted chicken enchilada? I thought she was fixing to come in her britches as she wolfed down a helping of chili verde as well. For she vowed that never in her born days had she tasted anything that exciting."

Glynis dryly remarked, "Then you took her home to make her come the other way, I'm sure, and the next time you took her to a Mexican place she said it wasn't the same."

He nodded and confessed, "That's about the size of it. The human mind is designed to stumble over pleasures and keep looking for them over the next hill. Nine out of ten hills hide nothing worth looking for. But where might we and Professor Darwin be if we stayed content to graze our short lives away in the same draw?"

Glynis didn't answer for a time. Then she said, "Try some of this French flan I ordered for dessert. It's surprisingly good for such a rustic setting, look you. Might you be suggesting that if we didn't have to part in the cold gray dawn, probably forever, I wouldn't be this hot for you?"

Longarm gently replied, "Ain't sure. It's hard to say for certain when you'll never know. Ships passing in the night have that advantage. No matter what they're really like behind the winking portholes, they'll always be remembered wistful."

His words inspired Glynis to set the tray aside, shove him on his back, and get on top. For a ship passing in the night, she rode every crest of his bounding main gracefully, and he found himself wishing they'd never have to part. For it was impossible to imagine anybody one lick prettier pleasuring him any finer. He felt sure that had she screwed any sweeter, it would have hurt.

So a good time was had by all until, as all things must, that one magic night in the Mountain Vista gave way to a cold gray dawn indeed, and so, once they'd warmed up a mite and enjoyed a bare-ass breakfast in bed, Longarm saw Glynis off for San Francisco at Uncle Pete's, and as they kissed on the platform, she swore she'd never forget him and he said he felt likewise.

He'd meant it too, being of mortal flesh with all its feelings. He figured she'd remember him at least as far as the South Pass, while he had to see that infernal banker before he got around to how he meant to explain last night to old Town-Taming Tess.

Longarm got the hired rig and its team out of the hotel's stable, tipping generously since Glynis had refused to let him pay his share of their stay upstairs. Then he drove back up Central Avenue to Drover's Savings and Loan, where this time he found T. S. Harrison in person, seated behind about an acre of desk and willing to talk to federal law.

Harrison said that thanks to bitching from his branch manager in Buffalo Ford, he was familiar with the cash problems Big Dick and his checkbook were inflicting on Kraft.

When Longarm repeated his question about things going smoother if Lord Bountiful wrote checks drawn on this bigger branch, Harrison made a wry face and said, "We've talked about that. Boss Whipple thinks the carpetbagger is deliberately out to cause arguments that are sure to be gossipped about by the Great Unwashed."

"Boss Whipple?" Longarm asked.

Harrison said, "Cattle baron and one of the directors of this bank. Pulls a lot of weight in the Wyoming Stock Growers Association, and has an overstuffed chair at the Cheyenne Social Club nobody else ever sits in. Did you know they have those new-fangled Edison lamps all along the veranda of the Cheyenne Social Club these days?"

Longarm said, "I heard. Ain't sure they're practical. You need all that telegraph wire and your own steam generating plant just to keep one of them Edison bulbs going bright as a candle you can buy for a penny and light with a match. Why might your Mr. Whipple suspects Wilcox wants folk gossiping about having trouble cashing his checks? Wouldn't they be happier if Branch Manager Kraft just handed over the cash with no delay or argument?"

Harrison nodded. "They would indeed, and Wilcox wouldn't raise half the dust for each buck. Kraft tells us Wilcox hands out his charity checks with considerable flourish as it is. So he gets a lot of noisy gratitude up front. Then the poor starving orphans are forced to wait a day or so unless some local saloon keeper is willing to be a sport about cashing their check, and so it goes, blah, blah, blah, with everybody involved telling everyone they know what a swell cuss Big Dick Wilcox would be, if only the current powers in Buffalo Ford Township would let him."

Longarm asked, "Can you tell me how much noisy charity and drinking money he's writ checks for so far?"

Harrison shrugged and said, "I'd have to look the exact figures up. If you'll take an estimate, let's say four to six thousand all told since he first breezed in this spring with the avowed intention of saving Buffalo Ford Township from the fairly decent administration they've had since the Grant machine was voted out."

Longarm hadn't had to wear a suit and tie on duty back

when old U.S. Grant, a swell soldier who drank too much for a president, had been in the catbird seat. But fair was fair, and things were running far less openly crooked under Rutherford B. Hayes, a lesser general whose First Lady, Miss Lemonade Lucy, didn't let him drink at all.

He said, "Then Big Dick's pockets may not be as deep as our side fears. I follow your drift about a heap of dust for every buck. But four to six thousand is more than *this* child has to spend on making himself look good. How do you suppose Big Dick or the sneaks backing his play mean to recover their investment? The taxing powers of the township council are pathetic next to those of the county and he ain't running for *county* office."

Harrison snorted, "He'd be swatted like a dung fly if he tried. He may not even win in Buffalo Ford, once people see through his flashy smoke and mirrors."

Longarm shrugged and said, "They only have to stay fooled a few more weeks. Eight in all. Could I have a gander at the sort of checks the cuss is handing out so freely, Mr. Harrison?"

The banker reached in a drawer as he noted, "Not really as freely as he'd have it known. We figure at the rate he's spending, they're holding him to a war chest of no more than twenty grand. We've only seen ten, so far, and most of it is still here in our own Cheyenne vaults."

Longarm accepted, and scanned the book of blank checks as he asked where Harrison suspected the other ten might be.

Harrison explained, "We've gotten letters of credit and certified cashier's checks from more than one bank well outside Wyoming Territory. All solid financial institutions, of course. But reluctant to discuss their own clients with us."

Longarm nodded and said, "Easy way to drag a red herring across your paper trail. I read his backers as a syndicate, seeing they bank more sneaky places than one. I notice there's nothing in the way of check numbers, account numbers, and such on these here checks. How come?"

The banker explained, "Wilcox has a special checking account with us, drawing no interest and costing him a nickel a check. The banking commission has been after us to number all accounts and issue checks so described, but think of the bodacious printing costs, and then consider we bearly break even when the customer writes in his account number!"

Longarm knew better than to ask why they let suckers apply for such accounts. They both knew that while the money backing a special checking account was in the bank, drawing no interest, the bank was free to play with it. But a lawman who worried about petty fibs wouldn't have time for the big ones. So Longarm tried, "What if somebody got saloon keepers and feed merchants used to signing this breed of check, then got his own ass in the district attorney's office, ran the experienced town law out of town, and then proceeded to paper the town?"

Harrison pursed his lips and said, "We've alerted our local branch to watch for something like that. How long do you imagine the gossip about a bounced check would take to spread through thirty-six square miles, or an hour's ride each way from the bank it bounced in? Con men have run that pony into the ground all over this country, Deputy Long. A professional paper hanger who establishes his face and some credit in town with modest honest transactions can, it's true, cash a lot of bum checks on a payday night and be gone when the banks open in the morning. But we're talking twenty here and as much as fifty there as payday night wears on. There's no way even a man used to handing out hundred-dollar checks could recover what he's already handed out in a flurry of paper hanging."

He let that sink in and grimly added, "As for his controlling the local legal consequences, that's why the voters

103

of Laramie County in their infinate wisdom elected a *sheriff* to protect them from such bullshit. Your criminal plans are just too pointlessly devious to be worth the trouble. Big Dick Wilcox or his backers want him to be the district attorney of Buffalo Ford Township and they want that real bad. It has to be something more profitable than a paper-hanging spree."

Longarm asked, "Can I hold on to these blank checks, Mr. Harrison?"

The banker said, "Be my guest. A good cigar would cost us as much. But I hope you see you'll have to start a special checking account with us before you make out one of those blanks for a dollar."

Longarm said, "You have my word I ain't out to sign my name to no bum checks. My boss would never approve. These blanks might come in handy for comparison, though, should I get to talking with some barkeep back in Buffalo Ford about a big spender."

Harrison frowned and demanded, "Are you suggesting Wilcox might be writing checks drawn on *other banks*?"

Longarm tucked the blank checks inside his frock coat as he replied, "Ain't suggesting nothing before I come up with some suggestions that make sense. My boss calls what I'm doing the process of eliminating."

Harrison snorted, "Allow me to eliminate that angle then. Were anyone to pay a bar tab with a check issued by another bank, neither this bank nor our branch in Buffalo Ford would cash it. Our tellers would see at a glance it was worthless, and so inform any townsperson trying to cash it!"

Longarm shrugged and replied, "So much for *that* elimination. Lord only knows what *else* I still have to eliminate!"

Chapter 12

Longarm got paid to keep his eyes open. So as he un-
tethered the team out front, he had to wonder what that
heavyset jasper was up to in that service doorway across
the avenue. He wasn't going in. He couldn't be taking a
piss on a busy street in broad day. So he had to be standing with his back to everyone like so because he didn't
want somebody to see him, and Longarm was the only
one on his side of Central Avenue with a view into that
service doorway.

Longarm climbed in, snapped the ribbons, and reined
east at the next corner north to head back for Buffalo Ford
at . . . say, quarter past eleven thanks to that warm farewell breakfast back at the hotel.

Having time to spare, knowing he'd arrive well before
dark if he dawdled, Longarm dawdled some to give anybody tailing him the chance to overtake him.

Nobody did. Longarm couldn't shake the feeling he
was being tailed, now that he'd spotted that shadow in
Cheyenne, but if he was, whoever they had doing it
knew his onions.

When he came to that cottonwood grove he and Glynis
had stopped to piss in, Longarm got down to lead the team

afoot off the trail, deep into the woods, where, sure enough, bluebottles were buzzing over a pretty little pile of turds.

He led the team on, clear to the far tree line, then tethered them to a cottonwood and eased back afoot toward the wagon trace with his six-gun out but pointed casually.

His ploy didn't pay off. Longarm stood there blowing smoke for the better part of an hour before an Indian couple in a one-horse shay favored him with worried looks in passing and he nodded in a friendly manner and called out, "Looking for mushrooms. I reckon this just ain't my day."

He went back for the team, informing the matched bays, "I'm just getting old and suspicious, or they feel no call to dog our hoofprints, seeing they know where we're headed."

Driving on at a faster pace, trotting them downslope and walking them up, Longarm made it back to Buffalo Ford just too late to pester Banker Kraft about his visit with Banker Harrison.

He figured it was likely just as well.

He returned the hired rig with its team to the livery and got his deposit back. Then he legged it back to Union Square to see if he could sneak some private talk with Town-Taming Tess.

He could. She sent her office boy out for coffee and donuts, and demanded to know where on earth he'd been the night before after promising her they'd make up for that quickie with the real thing at her place after dark.

He kissed her, seeing they were alone for the moment, and told her he'd had to stay over to interview Banker Harrison. It sure beat all how different she and Glynis Price-Jones could kiss and still be so friendly.

As their lips parted, for the moment, Tess pouted, "I'll bet you looked up a girl or more you know in the capital, you horny devil!"

Longarm assured her with a clear conscience he hadn't even been thinking about any female residents of Cheyenne since last they'd kissed in that very office.

Her office boy came back with the coffee and donuts too soon for them to risk another quickie, and Longarm was glad. It had been over eight hours since he'd taken it out of Glynis, but both the pretty little things seemed a tad more demanding than most, Lord love 'em.

Tess was smart enough to invite her hired help to share the late snack with them. He was smart enough to carry his out to the reception area, although he left it to Tess whether she wanted to shut her door again or not.

She left it open, knowing the kid couldn't follow her guarded drift as she and Longarm discussed election business and decided not to rock the boat for now by moving him out of the nearby hotel. He in turn intimated he meant to hire a pony and stock saddle over at the livery and maybe pay some calls across her thirty-six square miles. She allowed he'd be welcome to coffee and cake if he dropped by her place after business hours.

Aware that kid just outside the door was just outside the door, Longarm gravely asked Tess where her place was. She grinned like a kid swiping apples as she wrote it down for him on one of her calling cards. It was a caution how women seemed to enjoy such games.

Longarm had never had much use for *men* who enjoyed acting slick when they didn't have to. The fickle finger of Fate sent enough trouble a man had to lie his way around down the pike. Old boys who went out of their way to fuck a pal's woman, when you could get in enough trouble with the single ones, were assholes, in Longarm's book.

But thinking along those lines inspired Longarm to remark, as he dunked a donut while seated sedately across her desk from Tess, "Speaking from experience, jail cells across this land are occupied by the sort of folk who cause

107

trouble just to be causing trouble whilst they hug their fool selves for being so smart."

Tess nodded and said, "Tell me about them. I've lost track of how many fools I've prosecuted for roping and dragging an outhouse or making a minister dance with a six-shooter. Are you suggesting all this trouble I've been having with Big Dick and his boys might just be some sort of stupid *joke*?"

Washing down more donut, enjoying it more because he'd skipped his noon dinner, Longarm said, "Practical jokers have been known to go to some expense to set things up, albeit four to six thousand dollars and still counting does seem a mite steep for itching powder. I might be looking under the wrong wet rocks. But we can't eliminate him being just plain *loco en la cabeza* until we make certain. I know this head-examining doc in Denver who might know how you send out an all-points on escaped or recently bailed-out lunatics. I'll wire him the next time I pass your Western Union."

She grimaced and said, "I never considered someone else might want my crazy job just because they were *crazy*! But Big Dick has followers, and somebody must be backing him if he keeps replenishing his local bank accounts with funds from other parts. Do you often catch lunatics with well-heeled followers, Custis?"

He conceded, "Not often," and added, "When it happens, you often get to call the results a religion or political movement. I hear tell Mr. Karl Marx was living on the ragged edge over in Paris when this richer nut named Fred Engels grubstaked him to found that new Communist Movement. I don't even want to talk about the Fox sisters of York State, who raved about talking to dead folk and had grown men and women lined up to hear them babble. I'd best see if I can find out whether Big Dick subscribes to any Socialist ideas or the childish notions of old Single Tax George. I see I might have lots of such questions to

108

ask, and five cents a word seems steep. Reckon the U.S. Mails will see to the long shots well this side of November."

He didn't tell her, because there was no way she'd want to hear it, that Billy Vail had only given him a week off and he'd been up this way three days already!

Washing down the last of his donuts and jovially promising to drop by for coffee and cake if he ever got out her way, Longarm left to head back to Main Street. As he was passing their library, he saw that young honey blonde, Sue Ellen, wrestling with a carboard box big enough to use for a pirate's chest on the front veranda.

Longarm called out, "Save your back for the Harvest Dance and let a strong back and a weak mind give you a hand, Miss Sue Ellen!"

She wasn't dumb enough to argue. He suspected she was surprised as he was that half-a-dozen men hadn't already run over to give her a hand.

As he hefted what turned out to be a box of books, as he'd already surmised, the young girl explained some "big old sulky" as she put it had dropped the delivery off his dray and driven off without telling her they were out there, for land's sake.

Longarm suggested, "Maybe he has a bad back. This load's a mite more awkward than heavy. You lead the way and we'll follow you, ma'am."

She did. Longarm followed her inside and put the load on her counter, where, she explained, she'd put them in the stacks one at a time as she catalogued and made out inserts to go with each. So that would have been that had not Sue Ellen wistfully confided, "I'm not certain who might take me to the Harvest Dance this fall. Nobody I *like* has *asked* me yet!"

Longarm sidestepped gracefully by saying, "I'm sorry to say I won't be in town come September, Miss Sue Ellen. But it's a long ways off and I suspicion lots of swains ain't had time to study on a dance that far in the future. I'm surprised you've been asked at all this early, no offense."

She sighed and said, "None of the local boys *have* asked. That big old sulky Gordo Vance who dumped these books out front keeps saying if I don't go with him I don't get to go with nobody. But I don't *want* to 'tend the Harvest Dance with Gordo Vance. He's loud and fat and us Garths lost *kin* in the war riding for the Union Cav!"

Longarm suddenly realized. He asked, "Might we be speaking of a Texas rider who ought to lose about forty pounds? Works for Big Dick Wilcox, I thought?"

The librarian nodded and said, "Big Dick told Gordo and Knox to give Pop Newman at the freight office a hand when he heard Pop had hurt himself lifting. Big Dick's *nice* for a *Texan*. I 'spect Billy Knox has more respect for a girl than to toss things at her like he was slopping hogs! Gordo was all right until I told him I didn't aim to go to the Harvest Dance with him next month. But from the way he's carried on since, you'd think he was Mr. Romeo and I was refusing the part of his Miss Juliet!"

Longarm said, not unkindly, "Some poor souls get to writing plays instead of facing facts when the love bug bites 'em. Speaking as a lawman, I could tell you shocking tales of unexpected endings to such plays when others picked to play parts by the playwright don't say the lines he's written for 'em in his own head."

She gasped, "Heavens to Betsy! Nobody ever said nothing about anybody *loving* anybody! Like I said, he's loud and fat and from *Texas*!"

Longarm nodded, but said, "Do me a favor and tell your dad or any big brothers you got about Gordo Vance threatening any local swains who might ask. I'd have a word with Gordo for you, but he might not be the only one hereabouts who'd take that the wrong way, and like I said, I won't be around come the Harvest Dance."

Bidding the pretty little thing a brotherly farewell, Longarm went on over to Main Street to send that night letter to Denver General and, while he was at it, drop into a stationery store near his hotel.

He told the motherly old gent in charge—it wasn't the older man's fault he was aging so strange—that he was in the market for some envelopes and linen bond. He had no call to add he had some writing to do.

The old priss offered him a choice, and Longarm settled for some long serious-looking envelopes such as lawyers used to scare folks when they sent letters threatening to sue. They only cost a little more, and Longarm liked to be taken seriously when he wrote to anybody. He got the stationery man to sell him a page of stamps while they were at it.

When the older man suggested special delivery stamps, Longarm pointed out he could pay Western Union their infernal day rates if he was in a serious hurry. He said, "Plain old U.S. Mail will get a letter most anywhere within the month, and since I won't be here that long, I got to put my Denver reurn address on these envelopes to begin with."

The old-timer said, "We can *print* your return address on our letter press in the back for less than a dollar!"

Longarm allowed he'd think about that, and left with his purchases.

The more he thought about it, the less he cottoned to the notion of any return address in any way, shape or form. When you got your message across to the one you were writing to, there was no call to have your message returned to your address. In the event nobody was there to read what you'd written, there was no sense causing extra work for the postmen, or postal inspectors, who had no infernal business with such . . . informal corespondence. It wasn't as if he was fixing to send French postcards through the U.S. Mails, for Pete's sake.

111

When he got to his hotel, they told him he had a message in his box behind the desk. The clerk couldn't or wouldn't rightly say who might have left it.

As he carried it upstairs with his purchases from the stationery store, Longarm saw somebody had spent way more on their envelopes.

This one was pale lavender, scented with real attar of roses. He knew it was meant to impress him in a ladylike way. It still reminded him of a New Orleans whorehouse on a warm muggy night.

Carrying his modest load along the corridor, he spotted the match stem on the hall runner long before he reached the door of his hired room.

That wasn't where he'd wedged it on his way out. Somebody had been in there while he'd been out.

It happened that way now and again. That was why he'd gotten in the habit of setting that simple but effective burglar alarm.

Tucking the perfumed letter in with the stationery he'd just picked up down the street, Longarm quietly set the package on the floor, drew his .44-40, took a deep breath, and gingerly tried the knob. The door wasn't locked.

So the question before the house was whether his uninvited visitor had tossed his saddlebags for fun and profit before leaving, or was sitting there like a big-ass bird with his own gun trained on the hall door.

There was only one way to find out. Longarm twisted the knob with his left fist, and followed the muzzle of the six-gun in his right fist as he flung the door open to throw down on the figure near the bed as he snapped, "Freeze! You cocksucker! Move one hair on your chinny chin-chin and I'll blow your fucking head off!"

Then, as he saw nobody was about to give him any argument, all the red-faced Longarm could come up with was, "Sorry, ma'am. I thought you were somebody else!"

112

Chapter 13

Later, looking back on what a fool he'd felt like, Longarm would wryly recall how pale-faced an Indian chambermaid could get as she stared into the muzzle of a six-gun with a feather duster in one hand and fresh soap and towels for the corner washstand in the other.

As Longarm put his gun away, the blood came back up into her face, and she didn't sound pleased with his apologies as she politely but firmly declared, "Hear me, when others staying here do not wish anyone to enter their rooms, they hang that DON'T DISTURB sign hanging from the inside doorknob on the outside doorknob. Who did you think was in here? Are you running from the men who wear iron on their chests?"

Longarm smiled sheepishly and assured her he wasn't wanted by the law. She sniffed and tossed the soap and towels on the bed as she cut around him to let him work it out on his own.

Longarm stepped out in the hall to pick up his package. A not-bad-looking brunette was regarding him from across the hall, calm as a well-fed house cat as she stood in her own doorway wearing not all that much under her black kimono with gold dragons crawling up and down

113

it. He could see how little she wore under it because her kimono was hanging open sort of strategically.

As he picked up his package, he ticked his hat brim to her and said, "Sorry about that cussing, ma'am. I thought I was about to be shot just now."

When she didn't answer, but just kept staring like a house cat, he ducked into his own hired room and shut the damned door.

He put his purchases on the dresser, sat on the bed, and tore open the fancy envelope to read the cramped feminine handwriting in purple ink before he smiled crookedly and marveled, "It surely is a small world until you consider San Antone's about twelve hundred miles from here by crow."

Miss Foxy Burroughs had written it would be dangerous for them to meet there in town, even if Town-Taming Tess allowed such meetings. She warned him her house of ill repute south of Crow Creek could be under observation by mutual enemies, and suggested it might be safest to meet at the soddy of their mutual friend, Freehand Frank McClerich, after dark. Foxy said Frank and his Prairie Rose raised their pigs and chickens within rifle shot across from her own establishment on Red-Light Row.

The sly old bawd hadn't intimated why she wanted to meet with the law at this late date. But the odds were better than even she wasn't out to get him killed.

They went back to the time Longarm had saved old Foxy's bony ass when they'd locked up the wrong woman for a whorehouse killing just because the killing had taken place in her whorehouse, down in San Antone.

Longarm had taken the time to appear at her trial in her defense for the simple reason that he'd had to. A peace officer was sworn to uphold the law as well as the order, and the law said you weren't supposed to hang a woman just for being an ugly old whore.

114

From the way Foxy and all those other whores had carried on when he took the stand to testify in her behalf, you'd have thought he'd walked into the courtroom on water with a halo above his head.

He'd had a time convincing more than one of them that fair was fair and he didn't feel he really deserved to be kissed all over at once by a corporal's squad of naked ladies.

Reading the terse message over as he lit a cheroot by the window, he decided old Foxy was more likely to feel she owed him information more than a bullet in the dark. But was it smart to head out into the dark alone without telling anybody where he was headed?

He decided it was safer to trust old Foxy Burroughs than anybody he hadn't known as long. On the surface, it sure looked as if Portia Parkhurst's pal was really in trouble, backed by likeable gents Longarm had no call to distrust. But he was dammit *missing* something. Big Dick Wilcox had to be the sunlit tip of a massive murky iceberg with darker motives than the usual political hackery.

He set Foxy's mysterious message aside, resolved to go it alone for now since the more you took into your trust, the more you had to worry about.

He heard voices out in the hall. They sounded sort of sneaky. He got up and moved over to the door, grabbing a hotel tumbler along the way. He placed the open end of the glass tumbler against the thinner paneling of his door and put his ear to the base.

It only helped a tad. But a tad was enough when you had good ears and a loudmouthed idiot in the hall was exclaiming, "Lord knows you sure are pretty, and a natural man such as I has natural feelings. But no offense, none of the places south of the creek charge anything like five dollars a shot!"

A purry voice Longarm assumed went along with a catlike expression boldly replied, "We're not south of the

115

creek now, are we? A girl such as I has to pay protection to make herself so . . . available. I'd *let* you for two dollars if it was only me, for to tell the truth, you're a nice young fellow and I'll bet you're a stud in bed."

Her prospective customer offered her three dollars for three ways. She said four was her bottom price, and suggested he come on in and have a seat on her bed while they talked about it.

Longarm waited until there wasn't a sound coming from out there. He cracked his door open to see her door was shut. Heading innocently to the crapper down the hall, he didn't pause the first time he passed. He took his leak and listened tighter on his way back.

They were going at it hot and heavy if he was any judge of bedsprings.

He continued on to his own room, more puzzled than inspired. Everyone from Portia down in Denver to the avowed *enemies* of Town-Taming Tess had assured him shit like that wasn't going on in Buffalo Ford.

So why were those bedsprings twanging like so in broad-ass daylight if Buffalo Ford was supposed to be so tame?

Shutting his own door and mixing himself a drink with a bottle from his saddlebag and the hotel's branch water, Longarm considered just packing it in.

Sipping some watered-down Maryland rye, Longarm muttered half out loud, "Let's face things as they are. Two small-town political cliques are out to win the coming election as best they can, and would you give a shit which side won if you hadn't spent more time in bed with the one side than the other? Old Tess is all right, and Lord knows you sure ain't about to screw Big Dick Wilcox. But after that, ain't all politicians cut from the same cloth?"

As if in answer to his muttered questions, Longarm heard more voices out in the hall. He didn't need to put

116

the tumbler against the paneling as a loud authoritative voice he recognized called out, "I'll *tell* you who this is, Billy Knox of the Flying T! This is Marshal Brenner, and if you don't open this damn door, I'll huff and I'll puff and I'll blow the fucker in!"

Another voice Longarm recognized as the room clerk's suggested a passkey might be easier on the woodwork.

Longarm cracked his own door ajar to witness the way things went from there. Old Brenner and two deputies Longarm didn't know pushed in the door as the room clerk got out of their way, and there came loud screams and the sounds of furniture turning over until it got quiet as hell for a spell.

Then a hangdog cowhand came out alone, buttoning up as he lit out down the hall as directed.

A few moments later Longarm saw Marshal Brenner had been compassionate enough to allow the cat-faced brunette to get dressed before he and his deputies led her out in the hall, one of the deputies packing a carpetbag for its pissing and moaning owner.

As they turned their backs to Longarm, he opened his door wider to hear her protesting, "They told me in Cheyenne it was all right to do business here in Buffalo Ford as long as you kept it off the street."

Brenner replied, not unkindly, "They told you wrong, ma'am. When our city ordinance reads no prostitution within the city limits, it don't make no exceptions, and what you were doing just now was prostitution. So you'd have had your choice of thirty days or thirty dollars if that fool kid, Billy, had been willing to bear witness."

"We were doing it for love!" she wailed.

As they approached the stairwell, Longarm heard the older lawman chuckle and confide, "Lucky for you he loves his dear old mamma too much to risk shocking her to death. We'll talk about the best way for all concerned when we get you on over to the office."

117

Longarm missed the rest of it. But the rest hardly mattered. It was rough justice, but it usually worked pretty well. Billy Knox would know better than to prowl through transient hotels looking to get laid. His dear old mamma would never know shit. That cat-faced hooker would know she'd been given a bum steer by a fool, or just as likely a troublemaker out to make the town law they had look bad.

Raising his drink in a silent toast, Longarm muttered, "I reckon I'm still in. Brenner knows what he's doing, and the bunch who lured that poor dumb whore to this hotel are purely mean bastards!"

He consulted his watch and swore. It was too late to start anything else in town and too early to head across the creek to his secret tryst with Foxy Burroughs.

But watching a fellow lawman do things right for a change had done wonders for his appetite, and he had plenty of time for a sit-down supper before sundown.

So he locked up as usual, sticking a fresh match stem in place under that bottom hinge, before he went down the stairs and out into the late afternoon sun to scout up a table at that place he'd eaten at before.

He was early. So they were glad to see him and willing to serve him anything they had on their menu at the table of his choice.

He was working on a T-bone smothered in chili con carne under two fried eggs when young Deputy Saul Tanner caught up with him. Sitting down across the table Longarm had chosen by the open doorway, the younger lawman asked right out, "Are you fixing to take Sue Ellen Garth to the Harvest Dance next month?"

Longarm replied, "Hang a wreath on your nose. Your brain just died inside. I ain't fixing to be here next *week*. If I was, that library gal is too young for *you*!"

Saul Tanner said, "That's what I said when Luke Waters told me you'd been sparking her this afternoon. Luke said he saw you and Sue Ellen shilly-shallying on the library steps and she was smiling at you."

Longarm snorted, "Did he tell you I was hefting forty pounds of infernal books? I swear to God that you can't bust a jar of olives on the walk in a town this size without it being reported as a wagon load of watermelons demolished by an express train by the time the gossip is an hour old!"

Forking a mouthful of grub, Longarm added, "Do us both a favor and get out of my face so's I can eat without puking! I have been in some small towns and I have seen me some small folk, but Buffalo Ford's entire population seems to have been behind the door when the brains were being passed out."

As the fool kid left, looking sheepish, Longarm called after him that Sue Ellen had intimated she was anxious to go to that dance with *some* damned body!

When he got to the livery, he asked the genial hostler he'd coped with earlier to hire him a good night rider with a center-fire stock saddle, seeing he had no roping in mind.

The older man asked if his pal, Mr. Brown, had caught up with him.

Longarm said, "Not yet. Didn't know old Brown was looking for me around here. Did he say what he wanted?"

The hostler said, "Just asked where you might be headed yesterday as you was heading out with that rig we leased you. Asked when you'd got back when he spied them bays in the corral this afternoon. Funny he ain't caught up with you after all this time."

Longarm said, "It sure is. If he comes by to ask where I might have gone this time, tell him I thought I'd ride

119

down across Crow Creek to see if what they say about Gopherhole Gloria could be true."

The hostler assured him, "It ain't. No human female could take a stud horse to the roots no matter what those old boys who paid to see it say they saw!"

Chapter 14

The night rider they picked out for Longarm was a roan mare with a white blaze. Her name was Tinker. They crossed the stirrup-deep ford as the stars were coming out seriously in a deep-purple sky in the dark of the moon. There were other riders on the wagon trace, but nobody howdied in the sheepish vicinity of Red Light Row. Old Foxy Burroughs had written her place was the next-to-last one south. So when they came to it, Longarm glanced about to see nobody else close enough to matter, and reined east across overgrazed open range until they came to a fenced-in quarter section where a yard dog was baying and a lamp had been lit in a window of the otherwise blacked-out sod house surrounded by pigpens and chicken coops with a fair-sized barn out back.

"That you, Longarm?" called a familiar male voice as Longarm rode in, ignoring the yard dog once he saw it was stoutly chained.

Longarm called back, "It is. I see you've trained your old redbone to sound off at anyone coming in at you after dark."

Freehand Frank opened the door all the way, outlined by the dim light inside, and declared, "You know it. With all them whores across the way, we get the damnedest uninvited visitors. Get down and come on inside. I'll tend to that pony. My Prairie Rose and Miss Foxy have the coffee and cake waiting on your expected arrival."

Longarm did as he was told. McClerich took the reins from him. Longarm went inside, where he found they'd pinned tarpaper over all but that one narrow window.

A hippopotamus in a blue polka-dot Mother Hubbard had taken the lamp from the window to place on a plank table closer to their cold Franklin stove and put up more tarpaper. Freehand Frank had mentioned his Prairie Rose having a weight problem, but Longarm assumed the reason they wanted so much privacy was the older and way skinnier woman at the table.

Foxy Burroughs and Glynis Price-Jones were both red-headed white women, but they might as well have spawned on differant worlds. Never a beauty to begin with, the scrawny old sharp-faced whore had gotten even less appealing since the last time Longarm had seen her in that Texas courtroom. She rose from the table and came to him as he ticked his hat. He was afraid she meant to kiss him, but she shook hands like a man and said, "Let's go outside and walk under the stars, handsome. What I have to tell you don't concern these children."

Daisy McClerich snapped, "Thanks a heap, you secretive thing!"

To spare her feelings, Longarm explained, "It's considered polite along the Owlhoot Trail not to saddle fellow riders with things the law might want to know and they don't need to, Miss Daisy."

Freehand Frank met them in the door to say he'd stalled Tinker with plenty of well water and timothy hay. He didn't seem as surprised as his woman that Foxy was leading Longarm outside by one hand. Daisy was the only one there unfamiliar with the customs of her new man's past.

As they got outside, that yard dog didn't make a peep. They had it trained for criminal enterprise. Still holding Longarm's hand, Foxy Burroughs led him upwind into a corner of the bob-wire fence as she confided, "Dirty Dolores Delgado is a lying troublemaker, and the last time she caused me a night's sleep down Texas way, I warned her I would snatch her bald-headed if she ever lied to me again! But now I suspect she's lying again and I thought you'd *know*."

Longarm fished out two cheroots as he replied, "Hard to say, seeing I have never had the honor of knowing her from a barb on this fence, Miss Foxy."

The bawdy redhead said, "She even lies about the business we're in. Like I told you down in Texas, if I *liked* what unshaven cowboys want to do to me, I wouldn't charge 'em so much. But Dirty Dolores says I like to suck cock, and that Gopherhole Gloria's built so loose because her own father broke her in at the age of four."

As she accepted the smoke with a silent nod of thanks, she went on. "Gopherhole Gloria's mamma was never certain which customer might have been her daddy. Old Glory told me this herself when she asked if that was true about me offering group rates to them schoolboys. Dirty Dolores can't help lying when the truth is in her favor."

Longarm thumbnailed a match for the both of them as he quietly but firmly asked, "Miss Foxy, could we get to the point? Everybody lies some. Freehand Frank, inside, assured me earlier his Prairie Rose has never even suspected his outlaw past."

She got her own smoke going, coughed, and said, "You might have warned me we were smoking hickory sticks. Old Frank's gone straight enough these days unless you count short-weighting butter a crime. I ain't accusing Dirty Dolores Delgado of the *usual* lies, and . . . Don't glare at me like that, handsome. To make it short, Dirty Dolores has told me and other business girls she's collecting campaign funds for Town-Taming Tess to keep Big Dick Wilcox from getting elected and running us all out of Buffalo Ford."

Longarm felt no call to say he'd heard nothing like that from the district attorney who'd been sharing more than secrets with him. He said, "Nobody can run you ladies out of Buffalo Ford. None of you are *in* Buffalo Ford."

Foxy Burroughs said, "That's what I told Dirty Dolores. She says Big Dick's been promising to extend the township limits all the way south to the Colorado line. Can he do that?"

Longarm said, "Not without the approval of the county board of supervisors, and ain't you ladies already paying property tax to Laramie County?"

She sniffed, "We business girls don't discuss payoffs. Dirty Dolores says Big Dick surely has a heap of prospective voters convinced he can clean this corner of Wyoming up, as he puts it. That's what the spoilsports who won't even let their kids jerk off call frusterpating the shit out of 'em, cleaning up."

Longarm asked how much *dinero* Dirty Dolores was asking.

Foxy Burroughs said, "A thousand a house. Have you the least notion how many cowboys my girls would have to fuck and suck to raise me a thousand dollars? I run an honest house and let my girls keep half! I told Dirty Dolores I'd have to pitch in and put my own weary ass on sale to come up with that much money this side of roundup, and that was when she accused me of *liking* our trade."

Longarm took a long thoughtful drag on his smoke as he tried to make sense of what old Foxy had just said.

Foxy said, "Dirty Dolores says a woman ain't been serviced until she has two men sucking her tits, another man eating her pussy, and the fourth one coming in her

124

mouth. So I took her tales about Town-Taming Tess with a grain of salt."

Longarm asked what the notorious Texas troublemaker had said about a lady he meant to visit shortly. Foxy Burroughs replied, "She says the reason that female D.A. stands up for votes for women, and won't allow us working girls to even shop in her prissy town, is that Town-Taming Tess is one of those Lizzy gals who just hate to see other women fucking men."

Longarm laughed in spite of himself, and regretted it when the sly Foxy Burrough asked, "What's so funny? Might you know for a fact if Town-Taming Tess is a Lizzy gal or not?"

"Not hardly." Longarm lied, adding, "Just had a time picturing that, hearing *other* gossip about that towheaded lawyer gal."

"What do they say about her in town?" asked the older redhead with a vulpine leer.

Longarm said, "I ain't one for repeating gossip. Let's study on the campaign money Dirty Dolores is out to collect down this side of the creek. Is she asking for hard cash, or might she be willing to take a promissory note or check?"

Foxy Burroughs said, "Cash in steady hundred-dollar doses. She says she'll put all she collects in her own bank and write personal checks made out to Town-Taming Tess so's we'll have something to show the newpapers if she ever tries to double-cross us. I asked her how we'd get back at *her*, Dolores, if *she* turned out the double-crosser. She said if I didn't trust her, I'd be sorry when Big Dick Wilcox won!"

Longarm said he got the picture, which was only half-true, and when Foxy Burroughs asked what he meant to do about the whores across the ford from Buffalo Ford helping the D.A. of Buffalo Ford on the sly, he told her grudgingly, "I wish this wasn't true, Miss Foxy. But

125

there's no law preventing anybody for raising campaign funds for Single Tax George or the Irish Fennians if that be their pleasure. As for promises either way by politicians, politicians make the laws, and the day they pass a law holding anybody running for office to his campaign promises will be the day those pigs across the yard sprout wings and fly away as yon chickens greet the dawn with robin trills!"

"But what if we could prove she's *lying*?" the old whore insisted.

Longarm said, "Everybody lies, all the time. Lies are the grease that keep us from rubbing one another the wrong way. You can study all the statute books till you're blue in the face, and you'll never find a law against pure and simple lying. There are laws about obtaining money or a lady's favors with false promises. If you working girls chipped in to influence the election and the election didn't come out the way you all wanted, things are tough all over, but I reckon you could sue Dirty Dolores Delgado and get laughed out of court. Folk are always taking up collections for worthy causes or any number of one true gods. Common sense says there ought to be a law against such goings-on until common sense considers how much trouble sky pilots with the backing of their kings and queens have had proving the people they didn't approve of were lying. That's how come the Founding Fathers of this country put it in the Constitution that anybody can pass the hat for most any god or politician, see?"

She insisted it hardly seemed fair as they walked back to the house for the coffee and cake Daisy McClerich damned well expected to serve them if they didn't want her to feel too insulted to bear.

It was easier to see why Freehand Frank's Prairie Rose was sort of spread out as one washed her downright delicious pound cake made with more fresh eggs and butter than usual. As they munched politely, Freehand Frank modestly swore he had nothing further to add about Dirty Dolores, since such a happily married up man had few occasions to even cross the road to Red Light Row.

He said, "I carry shopping lists and the money they give me into town for Miss Foxy and some of her . . . business associates every now and then, since Marshal Brenner likes to arrest such ladies and make 'em pay a two-dollar fine if they upset the Christian ladies of the town. But I've never dealt with Dirty Dolores since she offered to pay me for my time and trouble with . . . In an indecent manner."

Longarm nodded knowingly as he thought back to that courtroom down San Antone way where one of the local beauties attending Foxy Burroughs's hearing had been pointed out as a Mexican spitfire who enjoyed her work.

Longarm could only picture a dark distant hat-dummy-pretty oval face with Spanish-spit curls and one of those lace mantillas rooster-combed above coal-black hair parted in the middle. He doubted he'd be certain she was *that* particular Mex spitfire if he woke up in bed with her come morning.

So when he left, Freehand Frank saying he'd see Foxy Burroughs on home, Longarm considered dropping by the wide-open establishment of Dirty Dolores to refresh his memory.

Then he considered someone else out there in the dark who'd been asking at the livery about his comings and goings. So as he mounted up to ride, he told old Tinker, "We don't have to go back exactly the way we came, Tink. We can ford Crow Creek as easy one place as another, and we ain't headed for the center of town just now in any case."

So they loped south across the short-grass under the stars for a spell before they swung west to circle Red Light Row and a chicken farm west of the wagon trace entirely, and forge north to ford Crow Creek a mile and a half upstream, hoping they were expected at the usual crossing.

Longarm rode north of the east-west trace to approach Tess Hayward's cottage on the edge of town out of nowhere expected. When she heard him riding in, she trimmed her lamp inside to greet him standing in her open doorway, naked as a jay.

Longarm held her close and kissed her fondly, as any man would have, but said, "Let me get my hired mount under cover with your mule in the carriage house before I tell you what I just found out south of the creek."

With most of her bare hide still pressed to his tobacco tweed, Tess drew back to demand, "What were you doing down on Red Light Row, you brute? Haven't I been all the woman a natural man might need? How could you even *look* at those painted bawds, knowing all the time I was out here ready and waiting!"

So there it was, like a streak of shit on the bottom sheet, and so he let go to step back and say, not unkindly, "It's been swell knowing you, Miss Tess, and I was hoping the magic would last us at least to the end of the week. But since I see it ain't, I'll just tell you what I think might be going on and be on my way back to Denver."

Tess grabbed for him, shoving her nearly white lap fuzz hard as she could against his tweed fly as she gasped, "What are you talking about? You can't be serious! You can't leave me hanging like this!"

He neither resisted nor responded as he calmly replied, "Sure I can. Billy Vail only gave us this week, but a week is enough when you ain't having fun. You ain't in any physical danger as I can see. There ain't no federal offenses I've been able to detect, and no offense, but you've commenced to nag."

She pleaded, "Can't a girl feel a little jealous while

128

she's been waiting half the night for her man to show up?"

He said, "Nope. I ain't your man. I was sent up here by a mutual pal to see if I could help a pal in trouble. I ain't saying I ain't enjoyed being a pal to you, Miss Tess. But fair is fair, and I wasn't the one who started us."

"That's a horrid way to put it!" she sobbed.

He said, "I never would have, if you hadn't nagged me past push to shove. But since I see we can't have us a civilized romance, and seeing I don't see anything I can do for you around here with my pants on, I reckon . . ."

"Would you take your pants off and tell me what you found out on Red Light Row if I blow you and promise never to ask about other women again for as long as I can get you to stay?" she asked.

So, being human, Longarm said he'd best put Tinker in her stall.

Chapter 15

Cuddled bare-ass as they shared a cheroot in the dark atop her bedcovers, Longarm brought Town-Taming Tess up to date on his visit to Freehand Frank's. She laughed like hell at the thought of whores she refused to abide in the shops of her town getting together to contribute to her re-election campaign.

Longarm said, "Miss Foxy said Dirty Dolores was a big fibber too. If I had the time and the postage, I could likely establish a link or more betwixt a Texas bank account of a former Texas whore and the constantly replenished special checking account of her fellow Texan Big Dick Wilcox. But since such transactions don't bust any statutes and go on all the time, you're as free to just publically accuse your opponent without being able to prove he's really being backed by the lower-lifes who resent you keeping Buffalo Ford so tame."

He took a drag on his cheroot and added, "He's going to call you a liar whether you can prove it or not."

She said, "Wait a minute! Are you saying Wilcox is a figurehead for the whores, gamblers, and receivers of stolen goods I put out of business when I was elected four years ago?"

Longarm grimaced and said, "Such folk never go out of business. They go underground until the heat dies down, and getting you dis-elected would cool things considerable in these parts."

She asked, "Wouldn't or *won't* the poor saps who vote Big Dick in on his flashy reform ticket be just furious with him when he breaks all those promises to clean up better than me?"

Longarm shrugged his bare shoulder under her tow head and replied, "They always are, the poor saps, election after election. They vote in a liar who promises to do good, and for the next four years him and his party does right well indeed, for themselves. So come the next election, the voters in their infinite wisdom elect another big fibber who vows to undo all the wrongs of the past four years, and sometimes he does, with his own new wrongs."

He took another drag, passed the smoke to her, and snorted smoke out both nostrils like a pissed-off bull to add, "Looking on the bright side, even if you lose, they'll surely want you back after four years of Big Dick running things wide open for a select minority of wilder folk."

She shook her head and said, "Not this child! If you think I mean to wither on the vine that long when I can hang out my shingle over in Cheyenne as a simple lawyer with connections, you've another think coming! If I say so myself, I've done a good job for the honest folk of this township, and if they want to vote the old ways back in, they are more than welcome to enjoy them because I shant be here, so there!"

She got so upset, Longarm had to make her come some more to calm her down, and she still pissed and moaned it wasn't fair. She asked if there wasn't anything he could do about Big Dick in spite of the sneaky son of a bitch coming at her perfecly legally with a dirty political campaign.

He patted her soft warm rump soothingly and replied,

"Ain't got but a few short days before I have to be back in Denver. If I had weeks more, I can't think of anything legal I could do to derail the four-flusher and his low-down backers."

She was as quick-thinking as most women. So she asked, "What could we do to stop him that might *not* be legal, dear heart?"

He sighed and asked, "Would you like 'em numerical or alphabetic? Mister Machiavelli wrote whole books on dirty politics, and political plotters ever since keep coming up with new ways."

Snuggling her naked charms closer as she lay her head on his bare shoulder, Longarm said, "False promises and show-off spending on the poor but deserving are run-of-the-mill and hardly worth comment if he didn't have such a bottomless war chest. Nobody ever runs on a platform of turning the hogs loose at the public treasury or charity for the rich. They just practice it once they get elected. You'll just have to convince folk your promises mean more. I don't see how you'd *outspend* him and his backers."

"What if we cut off the flow of his ready cash?" she suggested.

Longarm said, "You're in bed with a lawman, not a bank robber, Miss Tess. Neither Banker Harrison in Cheyenne nor Banker Kraft here in town have done anything wrong by anybody. Banks by definition handle money honestly if the bankers know what's good for them. They hold the money in a special checking account until somebody presents a check drawn on that account, and then they cash said check. There's no honest way I can stop Big Dick from making out checks for your Sunday school teacher or Miss Dirty Dolores. Albeit I'm betting he's going to write his show-off checks to more worthy causes than Dirty Dolores, seeing some of the money's coming from her."

133

She started to cry on his shoulder. He let her, patting her bare shoulder and knowing it wasn't helping. She had every right to cry if her job meant all that much to her. But that was the way things went, and tears just went with any game where only one side at a time got to win. Mr. Marx and Mr. Engels kept writing that under *their* grand notions, nobody would have to compete and no bigwigs would be in charge and governments would somehow wither away.

Mr. Marx and Mr. Engels were likely full of shit.

In the morning, Tess fed him scrambled eggs and jellied toast in bed, asking him to lie low there until after she'd driven into town. So he did, and if the maid hanging clothes out to dry in the next yard wondered who that was leading a roan with a white blaze out of their D.A.'s carriage house, she never asked.

Seeing he had the time and some horsepower to help out, Longarm carried his own heavily laden McClellan saddle into town with him by bracing it on his left thigh with his rein arm around it and his gun hand free. It was only the most awkward way till you considered what might happen if he rode into trouble with his gun hand bracing the awkward load.

Longarm tethered Tinker out front and carried the Mc-Clellan and his Winchester '73 up to his hired room, noting the match stem he'd shoved under the bottom hinge was still in place. It was an old time-tested burglar alarm that had served him well in other parts.

Draping the McClellan over the foot of the bed, Longarm went back down, made certain there were no messages for him in the lobby, and rejoined Tinker out front to ride her back to the livery.

When they got there, the hostler on duty said a heavyset cuss in a dark blue shirt and Texas-crowned Stetson had just been there asking about him.

Longarm said, "I'm sorry I missed him. Seeing I'm

134

back and your town ain't that big, no offense, we'll likely meet up sooner or later."

He legged it over to the town marshal's layout, caught Marshal Brenner in, and confided his suspicions and fears to the older lawman as they consulted a fifth of bourbon filed under B.

Marshal Brenner smiled gamely and said, "Well, shit, I still have a herd to worry about if these assholes want to vote their town wide open again. We ain't got near the financial backing, and you say there's no way to keep Big Dick's dirty paws out of them deep, deep pockets?"

Longarm said, "No way legal. Rob his bank and you may as well just shoot the son of a bitch, facing all that hard time in any case."

Brenner sighed. "Seems a crying shame. What if we were to ask old Herb Kraft at the bank to delay Big Dick's checks even longer? If you spread this around I'll have to call you a liar, but old Herb has always been mighty fond of Miss Tess."

Longarm said, "I've been wondering why your local branch has been dragging its heels on cashing Big Dick's cheap flash. But as he told me the other day, not mentioning any admiration for anybody, you can only sit on a check so long if it's good. I see now why he's been trying to get Wilcox to write checks only payable in Cheyenne. I sort of misjudged old Herb, and after he'd given me a swell cigar."

Brenner said, "We all want to help Miss Tess, even when our thoughts are pure. She's been a good D.A. But I reckon we'll have to leave it up to the Lord and the unlikely common sense of our registered voters."

He brightened and asked, "Say, what if we were to pack the ballot boxes in some of the outlying polling places across the township?"

Longarm shook his head and said, "You're up against a professional politico smart enough to be playing just

135

inside the limits of winning dirty and going to jail. Big Dick and his pals have already considered ballot box stuffing and given up on it, hence the big spending. They figured, as you should be able to see, that your local election will be overseen by your *county* officials. Ain't I heard tell of a resident undersherrif somewhere here in Buffalo Ford?"

Brenner nodded and said, "Uncle Bill Miller of the Lazy Diamond. Now that you mention it, Uncle Bill and his riders did circle some during our last election out this way."

Longarm said, "There you go. Only thing that can save the bacon for our Miss Tess is an unreasonable amount of reason on the part of the voters or a terrible mistake on the part of Big Dick Wilcox betwixt now and November!"

They shook on that and parted friendly but resigned. It was too early to think about another meal, Longarm had decided to stay the hell away from their library, and he was tempted to just pack it in and bum a ride to Cheyenne and the next train south.

For the whole fool play had turned into one of those pointless drawing-room comedies written by some dude who'd lost track of the points he'd set out to make, and nobody was going to get killed or arrested whether Longarm hung on till the last hour Billy Vail had given him to work with or got up and left the theater.

He'd done that more than once along 17th Street down Denver way, and tried his damnedest to get that society gal with the light-brown hair to walk out on that play about the Lady of the Camellias, speaking of tedious dramatics. But he was afraid Tess would think he was still sore at her if he lit out on her early, and down Denver way old Portia was sure to probe why he hadn't stayed to the bitter end and gone down fighting. Trying to look like a gent to everybody sure could be a pain in the ass.

He killed some more of the morning visiting with the deputy coroner cum horse trader and vet, Doc Smiley.

Time killed was all he got out of the visit, although Doc Smiley was a friendly old cuss who liked to talk as he purged a sick colt. Laramie County was satisfied Laredo Nolan had gunned the late Caleb Ferris, and the formal coroner's inquest later in the month would be no more than that, a formality. Longarm wasn't required to attend, seeing he hadn't shot anybody and there were all those other witnesses.

Longarm was mildy surprised the county meant to dawdle so, until he reflected on how many other deaths you might average a month in such a good-sized corner of Wyoming, and he knew from sad courtroom duty how shit-for-brains lawyers were forever asking stays so they could appear further along when they weren't so busy.

Deciding to eat early, Longarm returned to that nice place with the table near the open doorway where a man might admire the grub and the passing scene at the same time.

He had no trouble getting that table, seeing nobody else was there that early. He ordered their special consisting of roast beef, buttered salsify, and fried potatoes. Longarm wasn't much on rabbit food, but you didn't see salsify on the menu much these days and the vegetable oysters, as they called salsify back in West-by-God-Virginia, carried him home to when eating had been more of an adventure.

Salsify looked like skinny white carrots, and didn't really taste like oysters. Folks just said that after they couldn't figure what in tarnation they were eating. Salsify had a taste of its own, like peas or corn or sweet potatoes. Nothing tasted like anything else when you cooked it properly.

Then Big Dick Wilcox was sitting across the table from him without ever asking for an invitation, and he was from Texas, for Gawd's sake. So he should have known there were places along the border when a man could get killed for sitting on the same *park bench* without asking *permiso*.

But Longarm just nodded and went on eating.

Big Dick said, "Down where I come from, it is the custom for a man bearing arms to leave the hammer of his six-gun riding on an empty chamber, lest he shoot himself in the foot by accident."

Longarm nodded and said, "We all carry five in the wheel, when we're sober or not loading up for a serious argument. Have you come all this way to tell me that?"

Big Dick said, "No. I wanted to tell you about this gun waddie down along the border. Had a habit of riling others and seemed to enjoy it. But being a realist, he loaded that empty chamber in his six-gun's wheel with a tightly rolled twenty-dollar bill."

Longarm said, "I've heard he carved notches on his grips for every man he shot too. The legend goes that on the day he finally met the quicker draw we all must meet someday, they used the rolled-up silver certificate in his six-gun to pay for his funeral."

Big Dick said that was about the way he'd heard it as he handed a green paper check across the table to Longarm.

It was made out to the undertaker up the way as payment for a tidy-up and pine coffin for the bearer. It was signed with a flourish by Big Dick without naming any dead "Bearer." Longarm put it away in the unlikely event it might be admissable in court as a death threat.

When he failed to deliver the lines written for him in the bigger man's dyed head, Big Dick said, "I wrote one out to Gordo Vance this morning when he told me he aimed to have it out with you over Miss Sue Ellen. I begged and pleaded with him not to cause any trouble here in Buffalo Ford. But Gordo's sworn to kill or be

138

killed if he meets up with you anywhere in town after sundown."

Longarm washed down some roast beef and salsify before he said, "Your fat bootlicker has naturally told lots of others here in town about our pending affair of honor?"

Big Dick smiled expansively and said, "He has. I told you it wasn't smart to step on toes."

Longarm smiled wolfishly and said, "When you're right you're right, and you just made yourself one hell of a mistake, Mr. Wilcox. For I don't issue such challenges like a pimple-faced kid. But I don't run from them either. So seeing you all just declared war on my innocent ass, you'd better cover your own."

Big Dick said, "Look here, Longarm. I only came to warn you, not to declare any war on anybody!"

Longarm smiled sweetly and said, "Did you hear me declare war or promise to show you how dirty dirty politics can get? I only warned you to cover your ass as I recall."

Chapter 16

Seeing he might be facing some heat and dust before the day was over, Longarm went back to the Box Elder and changed to his lighter denim outfit. He considered the Winchester, waving its stock at him from its saddle boot as if anxious to come out and play. He decided against the notion for now.

He consulted his pocket watch and muttered, "Aw, shit!" as he saw it was barely noon. He went back down to find things quiet on the streets of Buffalo Ford with so many folks having dinner.

He went to the public baths near the barbershop, and locked himself in to have a private tub soak, meaning to be a clean cadaver if he lost and using up close to an hour before the water got too cold to be worth it. Then he got out, put his duds and gun back on, and went out front to kill more time in the barbershop with the shave and a haircut he'd been putting off. There was nobody ahead of him, damn it, and he had the feeling the barber had heard. Because the fussy old cuss surely seemed to spook at the snips of his own nervous scissors as Longarm sat there with his .44-40 in his lap under the barber cloth.

Marshal Brenner came in, his own gun grips handier

since he'd left his frock coat at the office. Taking a stand near the open doorway, the town law said, "We just heard. I got four deputies on duty full time and four in reserve, with more I can deputize if need be. Say the word and we'll posse up and hunt him down."

Longarm replied, "On what charge? Falling in love? Moon calves out to impress the object of their desire are forever threatening to do wonders and eat cucumbers. I have played this brand of chess before. I got to give him the first move."

The barber suggested, "Or get out of town before sundown, and nobody in town with half a brain would fault you, Deputy Long! Lots of us grown men know how that kid game is played. It's rigged against the sane. Shoot first, and you can wind up charged with killing a poor misguided youth who was just talking. Shoot too late, and the fact that he'll likely hang won't do you a lick of good!"

Longarm said, "Don't take too much off the top."

The town law marveled, "Gordo Vance ain't no misguided kid. He's a grown man who ought to know no Wyoming court will ever buy his Texas tale of love everlasting for a kid librarian!"

Longarm mused, "I've been told the poor loon is really in a lather over the innocent Miss Sue Ellen. So Big Dick Wilcox may have pulled on that lever as he was naturally filling Gordo's fool head with tales of sugar plums, political pull, and money enough for Froggy to come courting on a white stallion. I doubt anybody riding for Big Dick has a law degree. I know *he* don't."

Young Saul Tanner came in with a Greener ten-gauge cradled over one arm to report, "Big Dick Wilcox, Laredo, Truman, and Knox just now left town! They saddled up and rode for Cheyenne to a party meeting, according to what they told the hands at the municipal corral!"

Longarm quietly observed, "You call that setting up an

iron-clad alibi. I told you I've played this brand of chess before."

Brenner growled, "I see through that move! Gordo has orders not to break cover before his boss and the others are well out of town. That means he'll feel free to move in most any time now!"

Saul Tanner said, "I heard tell he'd given Longarm here until sundown. I got Thompson and Russell out looking for the fat son of a bitch. He ain't anywheres around that cottage Big Dick hired as his headquarters, though."

Craning his neck to let the barber get at the nape, Longarm asked to be filled in on the cottage, explaining, "I figured he was holed up in one of the other hotels in town."

Marshal Brenner said, "Ain't but two, and you're in the best one. Big Dick and his bunch stayed in the Box Elder when they first rode in this spring like they owned the town. Didn't take 'em long to hire the old Powell place over to the southeast. Graham Powell was raising bees and leghorns in that soddy till he got too sick. He was an old widower when he settled there. Dutch Vogler as owns the card house bought the property for the back taxes and hires it out when he can."

Longarm made a mental note that Vogler, like Delgado, might be easier than some for clerks handling bank transfers to remember. But all he said about the place was, "Gordo has to be an asshole. But I'm sure Big Dick and a professional like Laredo will have warned him everybody on our side will expect to spot him around his usual haunts in town."

Marshal Brenner opined, "He's holed up tight indoors where nobody but his own pals have ever seen him. He gave you till after sundown for his own sneaky reasons. It wasn't because he's a good sport. He hopes that like the professor here just said, a responsible adult who don't even hail from these parts might just leave town sensible,

143

knowing no other grown-ups would fault him, and clearing the decks for Big Dick with nobody getting hurt at all!"

Young Tanner asked what the other reasons might be.

Brenner said, "Even an asshole knows better than to walk down any street or along any alley to a gunfight in broad daylight. He'll come out like an armed and dangerous cuckoo bird after it's good and dark out."

Tanner asked, "Won't that make it tougher to find his target?"

The two older lawmen exchanged glances. Longarm said, "His boss and *known* cohorts rode out of town to establish an alibi. More than half the tinhorns Miss Tess Hayward has you gents keeping a lid on would be proud to steer Gordo and his gun my way, no matter where I make my stand or fort up."

Saul Tanner said, "Oh."

With two other lawmen standing by, Longarm felt it safe to have that luxurious store-bought shave. As he lay there under a hot towel, he heard a familiar voice asking Brenner if he'd seen that Denver lawman, Longarm.

It was that portly white-haired branch manager for Drover's Savings and Loan, Herbert Kraft.

As Longarm sat up, telling the barber they could skip the shave, Kraft said, "I just heard Gordo Vance challenged you to an affair of honor over the Garth girl, Sue Ellen. I thought you ought to know."

Longarm smiled crookedly and said, "Hell, Herbert, I knew that before you did!"

Kraft flustered, "Not *why* he was gunning for you over Sue Ellen, damn it. I thought you ought to know Gordo Vance, or his boss, Big Dick Wilcox, paid off the mortgage on the Garth family homestead over a month before you ever got here! Wilcox signed the check, of course. I understand Gordo Vance had the pleasure of presenting her with the clear title to her family property at the library."

Longarm whistled and said, "It's no wonder the poor sap is so mixed up about young Miss Sue Ellen. She told me herself she turned him down cold when he asked if he could take her to your Harvest Dance."

Saul Tanner gasped, "You mean sweet little Sue Ellen played that Texas gunslinger for a sucker? Flirted mortgage money out of a man only to refuse to even *dance* with him?"

Longarm said, "I mean to ask her next time I see her."

He turned to ask Kraft how much money they were talking about.

The banker said, "Five hundred dollars. The Garths proved their homestead claim year before last. Roger Garth mortgaged it for five hundred to make improvements that may not have panned out. I've had to grant them more than one extension, at higher interest, of course. I wish people would read the print on the loan applications they sign. We're not in business to *lose* money, no matter what Frank and Jesse think."

Longarm thanked the banker for information possibly worth following up on. Although federal lawmen trying to do much about gold-digging honey blondes would hardly have time to go after anyone else.

The somewhat older and far softer-looking banker shifted his not-inconsiderable weight and awkwardly volunteered, "I know some water's flown under the bridge since the war, Deputy Long, but I was a line officer in the Second Colorado Cavalry and I killed my Texan down at the Battle of Glorieta."

Longarm said, "I disremember what I did in the war. It was so long ago and we were all so young and foolish."

"Are you offering to back our play, Herb?" asked Marshal Brenner.

The banker blushed like a schoolboy caught jerking off

and replied, "I guess. This town's been good to me, and I haven't anybody depending on me since my Martha died. I still have my cavalry revolver, chambered to take brass, of course, and I guess I can still hit the broad side of an even fatter Texan!"

Brenner murmured, "Longarm?"

Longarm told the barber they were done, and holstered his own six-gun as he got out of the chair to hold out a hand to the portly banker and, remembering something Brenner had said, told him, "It's an honor to have you aboard, Herb. But now I want you all to listen tight."

When he saw they all were, Longarm said, "Big Dick and me would both like to see this bullshit with Gordo settled tonight. Whether he's been flimflammed by a flim-flammer indeed, or paid off by a false friend with lots of money, Gordo's having second thoughts already. I told you I've played this game before. He's hoping the long dry day with ants crawling around under *my* skin as well might inspire me to leave. I don't want him losing his nerve when I don't. We're being watched by his pals, even as we speak, so if he hears I'm forted up too strong or backed by more than my own guns, he won't be coming. We will have given him the excuse to give Big Dick. So do you gents want to help me help Town-Taming Tess show Big Dick up, I'd like you two, Warren and Saul, to make sure no kids come out to play after dark as news of the impending action gets around. Can you do it?"

The two lawmen said they guessed. Banker Kraft asked what he could do if he wasn't allowed to backshoot Gordo Vance.

Taking his hat from the hook, Longarm said, "I ain't the real target of Gordo's boss. I don't know how much Big Dick knows of her personal habits, but he surely knows where she lives and I can only watch one back at a time. Are you packing that old horse pistol you mentioned, or did you leave it at the bank?"

Kraft opened his summer-weight frock coat to expose the staghorn of a shoulder-holstered Patterson Colt .45, and it was sort of odd the way a gun that size made a portly white-haired cuss in a suit look so worthy of wary respect.

Longarm payed off the barber and told Kraft, "I want you and me to go get Tess Hayward at her office now. Then it's up to you whether you carry her home to her place, your place, or any place she'll be behind locked doors with an armed man at her side. Are you game, Herb?"

From the way he was grinning, old Herb surely was. So they parted company out front with the local lawmen and headed for Union Square.

Longarm never asked about matters he felt were none of his business, but along the way Herb Kraft confided he'd just admired the shit out of little Town-Taming Tess before she'd tamed his town. When he added in a defeated tone he felt too old and fat to even try, Longarm managed not to make a cynical remark about how old and fat rich men looked to your average ambitious woman. It was nobody's fault. It was Professor Darwin's revolution that having the power to provide was, for men, what antlers were for elk or tits were for women.

They'd barely made the open square when Town-Taming Tess tore across the tawny lawn on foot to meet them, shouting, "Custis! Have you gone mad?" and then she was in his arms with a casual "Evening, Mr. Kraft" aside to old Herb.

As Tess commenced to babble about Gordo Vance, Longarm shot a look around and said, "This is neither the time nor place for a conversation. Let's all duck into yonder library!"

They did, to find Sue Ellen Garth looking worried in the company of two young cowboys she introduced as her kid brothers. As Longarm shook with them, the older one said, "Pa sent us to fetch Sue Ellen home when we heard Gordo Vance had sworn to kill the man who's stolen his beloved. Sue Ellen here just told us you never even asked her to save you a two-step at the Harvest Dance. Is he crazy or what?"

Longarm said, "Crazy or paid off. But speaking of his motives . . ."

He turned to the honey blonde they were guarding to cock a brow and ask, "How come you never mentioned Gordo handing you free title to your family homestead when you were telling me about him pestering you, Miss Sue Ellen?"

She dimpled, and replied with the vicious innocence of the young and beautiful, "What if he *did* just deliver an envelope sent by Big Dick Wilcox? Am I supposed to fall in love with delivery boys? Our dad was mighty pleased when I brought the papers home to him that evening. He said he meant to vote for Big Dick, no offense, Miss Tess."

Tess said none taken, looking wistfully sorry for the younger gal.

Sue Ellen commenced to babble on about Gordo acting like more of a pain after just doing as he'd been told, but Longarm told them all he was running low on time, and suggested they all stay put until he was well clear of the library.

When Tess asked where he was going, he said, "I ain't certain. But I have almost an hour of daylight left to work with, and like the old church song goes, farther along we'll know more about it."

As he retraced his steps to the oddly deserted-looking main street, Longarm considered his options as his shadow strode ever longer ahead of him. If he forted up at his hotel, Gordo would never get up enough nerve. The card house for certain, and likely more than half the other bright spots open after sundown, were owned and operated by secret pals of Big Dick Wilcox, as anxious as their political figurehead to see the last of a loose cannon Big Dick could neither fool nor shut up.

As he reached Main Street, Freehand Frank McClerich hissed at him from between the corners of two frame shops. When Longarm joined the petty crook in the slot, Freehand Frank said, "I've never been much for fighting. My hands are too delicate and I've never even killed me an Indian. But if you need a place with thick sod walls to hole up . . ."

Longarm said, "Thanks, pard. I might call on you for help of another nature before I leave town by my own will in a few days. Right now I want you to stand well clear. This is betwixt me and Gordo alone."

Freehand Frank said, "No, it ain't. I don't know where he might be right now, but another pal who dwells down by Crow Creek says he saw Gordo Vance leaving the Powell place a few hours back with a scope-sighted Springfield .45-70. I don't think he's looking for a *mano a mano* with anybody. I think he means to pick you off with that high-powered sniper's rifle as you mosey about looking for him in the cool shades of evening!"

Chapter 17

After Longarm sent Freehand Frank packing, he smoked a cheroot all the way down in that slot as he studied on the news about that sniper's rifle. It meant Gordo might already be perched in some point of vantage, most likely covering Main Street and the entrance to the Box Elder. Gordo would have no call to snipe anybody leaving town by way of the municipal corral, as directed.

Had it been just himself and Gordo, Longarm would have been sore tempted. He'd walked away from more than one fight with a known asshole in his day, with nobody the wiser but other assholes dumb as a bragging jackass. But whether Gordo knew it or not, the declared war was not between the two left in town by Big Dick to stalk one another. The war was between a lawman on his own time, choosing to accept the private invitation to a marginally legal dance, and the asshole who wanted to win dirty and figured he had to, no matter how the gunfight he'd set up turned out.

Since nobody could be as slick as Big Dick thought he was, Longarm was ahead of him on the only two outcomes of the evening's entertainment Big Dick had arranged.

Big Dick was hoping Gordo might kill him, Longarm

knew, or failing that, saddle him with a confounded coroner's inquest in Cheyenne, thus putting Longarm out of the way for the few days Billy Vail was allowing for some damned resolution up this way.

It was too late to kick himself, now, for letting at least one two-faced cocksucker learn he only had what was left of a week in town.

Longarm finished his smoke, ground it out in the dust with a boot heel, and decided, "Well, seeing we're likely to wind up swapping shots with a scoped Springfield, we'd best continue this game with that old saddle gun we left at the hotel with our saddle. Oliver Winchester's '73 repeating lever-action can't shoot as far or accurate as one of them single-action Army rifles, but it's still a *repeater* that can lob a whole lot of lead whilst a sniper's reloading his Springfield, and what the hell, he might just miss me with his first shot."

Longarm started to step out of the slot and head on for his hotel. Then he wondered why he'd ever want to do a thing like that, and crawfished all the way back between the shops, past their shit house and carriage houses, into the north-south alleyway up the center of their block.

This educated Chinese lady who'd tried to teach Longarm to eat with chopsticks in bed one time had bragged on her own kind having some unknown science involving the directions you set a building on its foundations. Longarm had tried in vain to assure her that self-taught boomtown architects knew you laid out towns in the sunny-as-hell Far West with the directions of sunrise and sunset in mind.

She hadn't listened, calling him her adorable barbarian as they set their rice bowls aside a spell. But just as usual, the gents who'd laid out Buffalo Ford had oriented all the buildings they could to face due east or west, with doors and windows opening on north-south streets or alleyways, because that was the way you got the best hold on the morning or afternoon sun. It was best to site bedrooms

152

facing the sunrise so as to wake folks cheerfully and cool off all afternoon with the hot afternoon sun baking the far side of the building. Shop rents were higher on the west side of the street because that was the shady side of the street all afternoon, and nobody wanted to shop on the hot and dusty side unless it was for something serious like seeds or bob wire. Hence, as Longarm had just recalled, the entrance to the lobby of the Box Elder, like his hired room above it, faced Main Street from the shady side, and this alley he was following north would take him to their stable, backyard, and rear entrance.

He still cast a wary eye on a water tank overlooking the one wide intersection he had to cross. But as he'd hoped, not even Gordo Vance had been dumb enough to climb up there in the unlikely event his man might cross that side street some time or other. Gordo and that Army rifle would be covering some bottleneck where a visiting lawman prowling the center of town might be expected to expose his fool self.

As he took a deep breath in the alley and crossed the backyard fast, Longarm reflected on how far and how hard-hitting a .45-70 round was, next to the pissy .45-short pistol round with half the kick or stopping power of the .44-40 rounds a serious lawman favored.

The Army was forever recruiting greenhorns off the docks who'd never fired a gun, and it hurt their little hands and made them flinch when they fired a man-sized pissolivier. They got to brace the heavier recoil of their more serious Springfields against their shoulders, and that evened things out to where, in spite of such grim results as Little Big Horn, the War Department kept aiming single-shot but deadly Springfields at Mister Lo, the Poor Indian, to bust his ass at ranges he couldn't hope to reach with his trading-post repeaters.

But as he moved up the back stairs of the Box Elder without running into any of the hired help, Longarm reflected that range would be less important than accuracy at the ranges at which he and Gordo were likely to wind up swapping lead. So the real advantage Gordo had was the element of surprise combined with that fucking telescope sight. A rifleman who could miss with a scoped rifle of his own choosing at any sensible range inside the built-up parts of Buffalo Ford would have to be drunk or a piss-poor shot to begin with.

"It's a shame we never brought along a bag of marbles," Longarm muttered under his breath as he climbed the stairs. "For if there was ever a time to pick up our marbles and go home, this would be it!"

But of course he just kept climbing and meeting nobody on his own floor, headed along the gloomy corridor as, outside, the late-afternoon light was turning a pretty shade of peach.

But there was still enough light for Longarm to make out the match stem on the runner near the door of his hired room, and Longarm froze in place and drew his six-gun as he muttered, "Well, shit, of course!"

He eased foreward along the wall to his left with his muzzle aimed at his own hired door, feeling sort of dumb, now that he studied on the mental processes of a dullard armed with a Springfield .45-70 and Gypsy cunning. He'd been *told* Gordo Vance had stayed at this very hotel when they'd first arrived, and the way it was laid out was not as a devious maze. Gordo and that scoped rifle would be at the window, covering the approaches up and down Main Street for a target sure to head for his own damned saddle for his saddlegun by sundown. Fat old Gordo had no call to sneak through town with an Army rifle if he meant to just wait in there with a six-gun trained on the door.

Or so Longarm could only hope, unless he turned and ran.

Since that wasn't Longarm's nature, he aimed the muzzle of his .44-40 about where he figured that front window would be, took a deep breath, and kicked high and hard as he could.

As the latched door splintered inward, the blue-shirted hatless fat man who'd been hunkered by the window across the room eeked like a gal and tried to swing the muzzle of his loaded and locked Army rifle all that way around in time.

Then Gordo Vance's time ran out as Longarm's six-gun barked thrice, and Gordo let go of the rifle to do a back-flop out the window and bounce off the overhang to land in the dusty street beyond the shaded walk with a considerable thud.

By the time Longarm had reloaded and made his way down to the street, a considerable crowd had already gathered around old Gordo, sort of like penguins admiring a beached whale.

"I knew you'd win," chortled the rat-faced Dutch Vogler, who owned the nearby card house and had to be backing Big Dick and his bunch.

Then Marshal Brenner and two deputies were there, telling everyone to back off and give the corpse some breathing room, dad blast it.

Meeting Longarm's eyes with a smile, the town law said, "I see you boys never waited for sundown. He was laying for you in your own quarters?"

Longarm glanced up at the rosy sky to reply, "Close enough to his deadline, I reckon. He'd have never gotten off with that bullshit about it being an affair of honor at this late date in the Reign of Her Majesty. So it's just as well only one of us had to die as Big Dick was hoping. How long do you reckon your county coroner might keep me tied up at the county seat?"

Marshal Brenner shrugged and said, "Ain't up to me to say. Seeing you're on good terms with our deputy coroner here in town, and I think I see him coming, they'll set a date for the hearing and you won't be confined no place in particular, seeing you're the law and everybody in town knew this dead bucket of lard had premeditated your assassination."

The horse doctor cum deputy coroner elbowed his way through the crowd with his medical bag to howdy Brenner and Longarm before he hunkered down beside the corpse, opened his bag, and took out his stethoscope, fitted the fork to his ears in the shade of his straw hat, placed the horn cup to Gordo's fat chest, and announced, "I do declare this man dead. Pending the autopsy the county will be paying for, I estimate the cause of death as all these bullet holes in his shirt. Did you shoot him, Longarm?"

Longarm modestly confessed, "I cannot tell a lie. I did it with my little six-gun. How long is the paperwork likely to take us, Doc?"

The deputy coroner shrugged and said, "They're still filing papers on that Caleb Ferris who died resisting arrest in the card house. The mills of the law grind slower than the mills of the gods. But I can ask them to expedite the one hearing you'll be required to attend in person. Just tell me a good day of the week for you to appear, and a court clerk I'm in with over in Cheyenne ought to be willing to work with us."

Longarm said he'd wait on that until he figured out what came next in the time he had left in Buffalo Ford. The deputy coroner asked Marshal Brenner to get somebody to carry the cadaver over to his horse hospital cum autopsy theater for him, and Longarm, being free to go, went back upstairs to tidy up and let folks lose track of him before he made his next move.

His next move would have been back to the livery if he'd been wearing his tweed pants. Since he wasn't, he helped the upstairs maid tidy up to kill some time. He and old Gordo hadn't made much of a mess between them, the window being wide open when Gordo had gone out of it. Longarm picked up and set aside the rifle as the

156

maid swept up tobacco ash Gordo had flicked on the rug, smoking nervously with his fat ass on the sill to peer out beyond the overhang. The maid seemed confused by Longarm's courtesy. She was a full-blood, likely thinking of herself as a Sparrow Hawk Person, although to the Great White Father and his B.I.A. she'd be a Crow if she was allowed to run loose in recently vacated Lakota Confederacy hunting ground.

She was young and pretty in a moonfaced way, and wore her long black hair pinned up like a white gal's to go with her black-and-white maid's uniform.

He wasn't the one to brag. She was the one who suddenly stared owl-eyed at him and announced in a sure and certain voice, "I know who you must be. A Wasichu mankiller who is still respectful of real people while standing tall and straight as a pine can only be Wasichu Wastey! The one who fights everybody fair!"

Longarm said, "Aw, mush," and reached in his jeans for a quarter tip for the trouble he'd put her to.

She stared down soberly at the silver in her free palm for a time before she said, "*Gwuss!* It is almost quitting time, and even if Wasichu Wastey is generous as they all say, I do not sell myself like a shameless Sha-hi'yenah! But can we fuck in one of the empty rooms up here? There will be no way to lock that door you kicked in before the locksmith fixes it."

Longarm started to assure her he'd only meant to tip her for the extra chores he'd saddled her with. Then he considered how light it still was outside, and the way so many gals took it personally when a man implied he wasn't just dying to throw them down and ravage the hell out of them. So he said that sounded like a grand notion, and asked her name as he followed her out and across the hall.

She told him she was a convert who'd been baptized Elizabeth Ann by the Black Robes, and allowed they called her Lizzy down below. She seemed delighted when Longarm decided in that case he'd always brag on her as Miss Beth of the Absaroki Nation. So she locked the door, dropped her broom and dustpan near the foot of the made-up bed, and beat him easily at flopping across it bare-ass because she'd been wearing so much less to begin with.

Once they were fornicating in an officially unoccupied room, a shade stuffier, but sort of romantic now that the sun was setting out yonder to paint the room and every-body in it with dramatic purple and orange light, Longarm was just as glad it had been too early to go back outside with the memories of that gunplay so fresh in the minds of friend and foe alike.

For the tawny and solidly built full-blood sure offered a swell change from the elfin Glynis and almost albino Tess. Picturing the whiter rump of Town-Taming Tess in the same situation as he dog-styled this tawny unexpected pleasure in the gloaming inspired him to hump so hard Beth laughed and called him her *tatanka woniya,* which was mighty flattering if Longarm was translating it right as something like the very spirit of a raging bull. So he turned her on her back to finish right as she stared up at him adoringly while panting in his face like a puppy Plains Indian-style.

By the time they'd finished a shared cheroot, it was fair dark out and she was a good sport, being from a warrior race, when Longarm told her he had to go back to war and she wasn't to count on any more such slap-and-tickle because he'd only be in town a few days and had a heap of bases to cover.

Beth kissed him and said, "Don't worry. I won't tell the district attorney you just fucked me, Wasichu Wastey. I have heard how you are always doing something to sur-prise others, and I am so happy you just chose to surprise me this way this day!"

158

Chapter 18

Longarm sloshed across Crow Creek in the dark in his boots and jeans without getting wet enough to matter. He strode on to Freehand Frank's, and when the small ex-convict responded to his yard dog's yapping with, "I've got a gun, whoever that might be out yonder!" the man seemed tickled when Longarm answered him with a remark about his brains.

As he hauled Longarm in out of the dark, Freehand Frank said, "I heard you won. But after that, nobody in town knew where you were, seeing you weren't in your hotel room nor nowheres else. So I come on home to tell my Daisy here how you'd won the war!"

Longarm ticked his hat brim to the lady of the house as he told her man, "That was *their* war. The war I declared ain't *started* yet. I got some letters to write and stamped envelopes to send out far and wide. I don't want my own handwriting presented as evidence later. So I'm asking you and Miss Daisy here to take down some dictating in your own handwriting because there is no way either of you could ever be connected with this opening maneuver of my own campaign."

Daisy stared down pensively at all the paper Longarm

had taken out of his pockets to spread across her table, and suggested heating up the pot and cutting open a fresh cake.

/ But in fact it didn't take them all that long to transcribe the terse but widespread communications Longarm had in mind. They were finished well before midnight, and Free-hand Frank said he'd be proud to carry the stamped en-velopes into town a few at a time over the next few days and just slip them through the post-office-door slot after hours in a way that shouldn't attract attention. The sly little cuss said he savvied why Longarm didn't want any-body else recalling just when a particular envelope might have been sent from Buffalo Ford.

By the time Longarm polished off more than enough rich pound cake to satisfy a normal healthy appetite, his jeans were dry, and if his socks were still a little wet, he had to wade back across the fool creek in any case. So, thanking his hosts for the coffee, cake, and other help, Longarm took his leave and headed back out to the wagon trace across the crunchy dry short-grass. The red lanterns and lit-up lace-curtained windows on the far side assured him the night was young for slap-and-tickle. Before he got to the bare wagon ruts, the doorway of one place exploded open to spew half-a-dozen likkered-up cow-hands and a bevy of soiled doves seeing them off safely, if not as rich as they'd commenced the evening.

Longarm just froze in place, aware he stood barely vis-ible, if at all, with the moonless open range at his back. So he was granted a free look at the four naked whores, and . . . Right. Even though he hadn't seen her bare ass in court that time down in San Antone, that had to be Dirty Dolores with the spit curls and the Spanish comb in her shiny black hair. She had bigger tits than he'd been giving her credit for.

As Dirty Dolores and her help waved their satisfied customers down the plank steps and aboard the ponies they'd tethered out front, Longarm grinned wolfishly and silently warned her, "Don't blame *me* when you get that letter from your bank in San Antone, Miss Dolores. It was your misfortune and none of my own that you chose to throw in with a total asshole who didn't know enough to leave me be when he was winning!"

The four whores turned their bare asses to him and went back inside.

Longarm continued on his way, cussing human nature as he tried to tell himself not one of those bare asses had been at all tempting. It hardly seemed fair, but all bare asses had some effect on all men, no matter whose bare ass they'd recently had their own wicked way with, and he could hardly wait to get on over to Tess Hayward's cottage and tell her how smart he'd just been while she was bare-ass.

It took a spell to walk that far with water squishing between your fool toes, and along the way he had time to reconsider just how much he ought to tell old Tess. She was an officer of the court, after all, and while he was working for her pro bono and off duty as a lawman, and didn't see how anyone could ever say he'd done anything *immoral*, he'd asked Frank and Daisy to address those envelopes and post them sneakily because he never wanted to have to explain just *bending* rules that might not be on the books. By the time he got there, he'd decided to just tell Tess he'd done all he could for her in the time Billy Vail had given him to do it.

He felt sure that since everyone in the township seemed to be such a gossip, Big Dick Wilcox knew when he'd be having to haul ass, and as soon as he learned his fighting cock had lost, he'd go to ground in Cheyenne and stay there till he felt it was safe to return to Buffalo Ford, the slithering slimy shit-worm.

A distant steeple clock was chiming eleven as Longarm turned into Tess Hayward's gate. She'd told him her latch

161

string would ever be out to him, but when he twisted the knob, nothing happened. So he knocked.

It took quite a spell, and when Tess cracked open the door, she was breathing funny in her kimono with her long tow hair unpinned. She stammered, "Oh, it's you. I wasn't expecting you at this hour and I fear you've, ah, caught me at an awkward time, Custis."

He didn't comment on the aroma of an American-made but expensive cigar hanging about her in the doorway. He said, "I'm sorry I woke you up, Miss Tess. I'll drop by your office in town before I leave town. It wasn't important enough to . . . wake a lady up."

As he turned away, Tess came out of the cottage after him, calling out, "Wait, Custis, where are you going at this hour and, oh, shit, if this isn't awkward!"

He just kept walking, not looking back as he knew she wouldn't follow far along the cinder path on her bare feet. An older and wiser hand he'd always been grateful to had told a once-raging younger Custis Long that nothing a man could say to a woman at such times beat just quietly walking away. She wailed something after him as he turned at her gatepost to head on back to his hotel, idly wondering, and wishing he didn't, whether old Herb Kraft's pubic hair was white as hers as they made up for lost time. He told himself not to be a poor sport, and had to laugh as the mental picture of Freehand Frank and all that Prairie Rose going at it the same way popped unbidden into his suddenly lonesome mind.

Getting to the Box Elder to find they'd repaired his busted door upstairs, Longarm reflected as he morosely got undressed that it had never killed a man to sleep alone after he'd already had some at sundown, for Pete's sake.

But he was still pleased as punch when there came a shy knock on the door and he opened it, half-dressed, to see little Elizabeth Ann of the Absaroki Nation standing there in her own kimono.

As he hauled her and barred the door, she explained she lived on the premises and she'd been hoping he might come back that night.

She wasn't used to kissing Wasichu-style, and said it tickled, but seemed to be getting used to it as Longarm pounded her hard with pictures of everyone from fat old Daisy McClerich to that bitty Chinese gal so interested in the science of positions.

When they finally had to come up for air, Beth laughed like a kid with a strange new toy and told him she'd been sure he meant to spend the night with that *paskaweya* he'd been fucking.

Hoping to undo some damage, Longarm tickled Beth's fancy with his free hand as he cuddled her close and said, "You shouldn't listen to such *tachesli*. I've been up here helping her keep her job as your district attorney. *Wasichun sika* who want to defeat her have been saying all sorts of things about her. Was it fair for your Lakota enemies to tell everybody the Sparrow Hawk Men slept with their own sisters?"

She swore in the dialect her kin shared with their worst enemies, and assured him no such thing had ever happened since Wakan Tanka carved the first stone pipe long ago and far away!

He said, "There you go. See you tell your pals I never spent this night with any blond women."

Beth allowed she meant to tell them where he'd spent the night, but asked how come he was going to so much trouble for a woman he wasn't sleeping with.

He confided, "I was starting to wonder that before Big Dick Wilcox invited me to a war dance. I came up here as a favor to another friend, and whilst I can't say I'm *sore* at Town-Taming Tess, I was commencing to feel there was nothing much I could do about the usual run for office as such runs are conducted across this land of opportunity. So had Big Dick just acted sensible until I

163

ran out of steam, I'd have no doubt packed it in and let the two sides fight it out dirty as usual."

He snuggled her closer and explained, "When a man sets out to get other men killed, that ain't just dirty. It's a public menace, and I am duty-bound to protect the public from deadly menaces."

They made love some more, and caught some sleep before Beth slipped out before dawn lest she get her sassy brown ass fired.

Longarm lay slugabed until the noise of traffic along Main Street told him business hours were in progress. He rolled out of bed, got cleaned up, and had breakfast at another beanery to keep in practice. For gents who ate every meal at the same table were as reckless as gents who sat with their backs to the doorway.

The morning was shaping up pretty for the dog days as Longarm made it over to the deputy coroner's. He found the old-timer putting drops in the eyes of a pup a snot-nosed but pretty little girl was holding. The old-timer sent them on their way, gratis, before he turned to his older caller with a weary smile. observing, "The lady of their house has a drinking problem and they both have fleas. The cause of death in the case of that Texan was mostly a ventricular septal defect he sustained by being shot through the heart. But his severed aorta never did him a lick of good, and you nailed him through his trachea with one round as well."

Longarm said, "I figured he might be dead. Came to talk to you about setting a date for the formal hearing at the county seat, Doc."

The sardonic but kindly old cuss said, "Just sent the remains on to Cheyenne with my preliminary findings. My boss has to live too. He'll cut my butcher's twine, have his own look-see, and sew the poor cuss back up. I included a note to that county pal I told you about. With any luck they'll impanel a coroner's jury next week and you'll be off the hook and free to go."

Longarm grimaced and said, "My boss is surely going to give me pure Ned for overstaying his deadline. But being a lawman himself, he'll see we had no choice and . . . Hold the thought, Doc!"

He counted in his head, nodded, and asked, "Is there any chance at all they could hold their formal hearing as late as next month? Late as around the time of that Harvest Dance?"

The deputy coroner said, "Sure, better late as hell is a comfortable speed for the mills of the law, and it ain't as if we're dealing with a mystery or a perpetrator apt to flee justice. That's what we call you when you shoot a cuss but ain't been charged yet, a perpetrator. It means the one who performed the act, in Law Latin."

Longarm dryly remarked, "So I've been told. How long will it take to find out whether I can appear at that hearing and make it to your Harvest Dance in the same run up from Denver, Doc?"

The old-timer said they could likely settle it that day if Longarm was willing to spring for the telegraph fees both ways. When he added the Western Union charged a nickel a word, Longarm said, "I know. I just used up a sheet of stamps. Why don't we stop off for a drink as long as we're headed that way this morning?"

Seeing he had no horse to doctor nor cadavers to cut open, the deputy coroner said he'd be proud to have that drink with Longarm.

They had drinks going and coming from the Western Union. When the older man said he figured on an answer by four if they got any answer at all, Longarm said he'd be back, and returned to the hotel to sign out before noon and save a day's hire of the room upstairs. He was glad he didn't run into the full-blooded and warm-natured Beth as he went up to fetch his saddle and shit. He was still wearing his more comfortable denim outfit, seeing he still had a wagon ride to bum into Cheyenne no matter how things turned out.

He carried his load over to the deputy coroner's, took off his denim jacket, and helped the older man wrestle a sick mare off her feet so she could be tapped for the bloat white lying down and hog-tied. Horses did raise Ned, next to cows, when you let all that fermented greenery rip.

Marshal Brenner joined them as they were soothing the mare, or trying to. Nothing female was all that easy to soothe after they'd worked themselves up to a hissy fit.

Brenner said, "Miss Tess has been asking for you, Longarm. What's this we hear about you leaving the Box Elder?"

Longarm said, "Had to. Won't be here this evening, and I ain't made of money. You reckon you could rustle me up a ride into Cheyenne as you make your rounds, Warren?"

Marshal Brenner said, "I guess, but how come you're leaving so sudden? Didn't you say you had a few days left?"

Longarm said, "Nothing up this way worth hanging around for, no offense. Can't arrest anybody for trying to buy votes with cheap flash and big money, even if Big Dick was here, which he ain't. I'd never prove he put Gordo up to that dumb gunplay, so there's no sense in my trying."

Brenner looked away and said, "Miss Tess intimated she's afraid you might be sore at her."

Longarm shook his head and said, "Tell her for me she ain't done a thing I might not have done in her place if I'd been a pragmatic gal. Tell her I just had to get it on down the pike for now no matter when they set the date for that hearing in Cheyenne. Tell her I might come by to help you all celebrate if Doc here can set me up with a hearing about the time of your Harvest Dance."

166

Brenner sighed, "What are we likely to have to celebrate with the election only weeks off if you pull out on us now?"

Longarm said, "I said I had to go back to Denver for now, Warren. I never said I was pulling out. Not for good leastways."

Chapter 19

Longarm caught a ride into Cheyenne to get there just after dark, and seeing Billy Vail was only going to put him to work if he showed up earlier than expected, Longarm hired a hotel room across from the U.P. Depot to store his shit, get washed, and dress more properly, then ambled across West 15th to see if Miss Beverly, slinging hash in the depot dining room, remembered him.

The pneumatic little thing sure did, and seeing she got off in about an hour, Longarm had time to see how he liked the new saloon in the new cast-iron Hoffman Building a couple of blocks west.

They served cold beer, chilled scientific by ammonia pipes. Longarm would have found the bar more pleasing had not Big Dick Wilcox in the flashy flesh bellied up to the bar beside him to observe, "I see you won. I take it you're in town for the county inquest?"

Longarm dryly answered, "Take it up your ass for all I care. Did you know that when we examined Gordo's six-gun his hammer was riding on an empty chamber? You never gave him that check you bragged on. You gave me one to scare me, and that was only *one* of the mistakes you made."

Big Dick answered innocently, "I don't know what you're talking about. If you think I've done anything you could possibly arrest me for, I'd like to see you try!"

Longarm said, "We both know you skate too slick across thin ice to bust all the way through, you gloating asshole, and when I call you an asshole, I am only stating a simple fact. Gordo Vance would be alive this evening, and I'd be fixing to leave for Denver without a hope of stopping you and your tinhorn backers from buying the fall election lawfully as the rules allow."

"You admit you're licked?" asked Big Dick with a smile.

Longarm said, "I admit there's nothing I can charge you with that would stick in court if your lawyer ain't as ignorant of the law and common sense as you. But you know what they say about he who laughs last, and you really need to cut down on practical jokes and jackass braying."

Big Dick asked if he could buy Longarm a drink, seeing their war was over and he was a gracious winner.

Longarm said, "I'm particular who I drink with. Why don't you go count your chickens before they hatch?"

Big Dick moved away, smiling at himself, and Longarm left the rest of his beer on the bar with the bad taste inspired by Big Dick.

Beverly cheered him up a lot when he picked her up after work, and they felt so good about that, he overstayed Billy Vail's deadline by a weekend.

But as all things must, good and bad, his time off ended, and old Billy worked his ass so hard when he got back to Denver, it took him some time to notice Portia Parkhurst, Attorney at Law, was avoiding him.

Rather than ask her what Town-Taming Tess had written or wired, he agreed to squire that young widow woman up on Sherman Street to her infernal shows and socials, seeing the dog days of summer were giving way to the cooler nights and balmy days of autumn on the high plains and seeing she sure got wild in bed for such

170

a prim and proper high society gal. When *she* hit him with questions about his visit with Town-Taming Tess, Tess being famous in Western female circles and gossip traveling fast as any wind across the high plains, Longarm was able to assure her truthfully that the last he'd heard, the lawyer gal still running for district attorney up in Wyoming had an understanding with the biggest banker in town. So she asked if he'd take her to see an English drawing-room comedy where he was sure nothing was going to strike him funny.

But Billy Vail saved the day by sending him down to Trinidad to pick up a federal want working as a coal miner, and that was another adventure that took weeks and got him laid three times, with one of them really pretty.

Then the nights were getting crisp enough to feel comfortable in suits and ties, and Portia Parkhurst, Attorney At Law, had sent him a perfumed note reading, "We have to talk! How did you ever *do* it?"

So Longarm went back to Billy's office to ask if he could leave a shade early that day, during business hours. Portia hadn't said she wanted him calling on her at home, and a younger gal with light-brown hair would be waiting supper on him that evening.

But old Billy grumped, "Hell, no, you can't have the rest of the day off, you lollygagging cuss! We just now got a subpoena from the coroner of Laramie County, Wyoming Territory, requiring your attendance before him and his jury on pain of prosecution! Why in thunder did you ever shoot that fucking Texican up yonder?"

Longarm innocently replied, "I told you when I first got back last month, the fucking Texican was waiting for me in my hotel room, aiming to shoot me. I know it's a pain in the ass to do without my sterling services whilst I go back north for that coroner's hearing, but think how much work I'd have done for you recent if I'd let old Gordo win!"

So his boss had to be a sport about it, and gave Longarm another week to get his ass on back to Wyoming and this time *settle* everything.

Longarm left that night without calling on Portia, but supping and swapping some spit up on Sherman before his night train left.

When he passed through the U.P. dining room, Beverly was jawing with a tall drink of water in expensive duds. When she turned red and looked away, Longarm kept walking. He knew how the poor gal felt.

A late night in bed alone after an earlier quickie didn't kill him, and the next morning at the courthouse they told him the hearing was set for the next day, leaving him better than twenty-four hours to kill, and he'd been planning his return around the Harvest Dance that night in Buffalo Ford.

He spent an educational morning in the public library, reading the back issues of local newspapers they had on hand. Then, seeing he was going to a dance, Longarm treated himself to a long hot soak, a sit-down shave, and a haircut, marveling it had been so long since that last trim the day of his showdown with Gordo Vance.

Back at his hotel, he put on fresh underwear and a clean shirt, then went down and hired a white horse and fancy stock saddle for a few dollars more, knowing everyone in Buffalo Ford would be staring at him and hoping some of them might be pretty.

The prancing white show hunter was sixteen hands high, and gave a comfortable ride at any gait with its long back and springy pasterns. They'd told him to call it Prince Charming, even though it was a gelding. Longarm wasn't one for giving fancy names to horses. So he just said, "Let's be on our way, pard," as they lit out for Buffalo Ford, loping some and walking some, to get into Buffalo Ford later that afternoon in time to pay a call on Marshal Brenner as custom dictated.

The first thing Warren Brenner said as he got out that

bottle was: "I don't know what in tarnation you did the last time you were up our way, but it sure worked swell! Big Dick's been hiding out from Laredo Nolan, they say. I can't prove it, so I don't have to arrest Laredo before he shoots the loudmouthed cocksucker."

Accepting his tumbler, Longarm soberly replied, "I ain't surprised the syndicate chose Laredo. We knew he was a professional shootist the night he swatted Calvin Ferris like a fly."

Brenner threw back his own red-eye, wheezed, and asked, "But why is he after his former boss now? He's supposed to be riding *for* Big Dick whilst all them townsfolk Big Dick stiffed with bum checks have it out with the flashy four-flusher! Did you and Herb Kraft at the bank do that, Longarm? I asked Herb, and he swears that whilst he's pleased as punch, he just can't say why drafts on the main branch came back marked insufficient funds. You didn't get Banker Harrison over at the main branch in Cheyenne to do anything sneaky, did you?"

Longarm shook his head and said, "Far as I know, Bankers Harrison and Kraft had nothing to do with Big Dick's overdrawing his special checking account. Bankers ain't allowed to mess with the deposits of their customers."

Then, since he didn't like to lie and knew he wasn't about to tell the local *law* what he'd pulled on Big Dick Wilcox, Longarm said he had to get his show hunter out of the late sun, and left before he had to fib to a pal.

He saw they rubbed Prince Charming down and watered him before they let him at that timothy, show hunters having more delicate stomachs than rough-and-ready cow ponies. He had over an hour to kill before that Harvest Dance commenced at sundown. Figuring it might be less awkward alone and personal than on a dance floor, Longarm strode over to Union Square to meet Town-Taming Tess and Herb Kraft coming the other way, arm in arm.

From both their awkward expressions, Longarm suspected old Tess, being a woman, had naturally had to tell old Herb he'd fucked her first. Longarm had never figured whether women did that confessing or bragging. She held out a hand and trilled, "Custis, it's so good to see you again! Are you in town for the dance?"

He shook hands with her as if she'd been a man, feeling sort of sorry for Big Dick as he replied, "Something like that. Had to come back north for that coroner's inquest in Cheyenne, and figured I'd drop by and see how things are in Buffalo Ford, Miss Tess."

Banker Kraft replied for them both with forced heartiness, "Things could not be going better, Longarm! You were so right about there being only so much money, and Wilcox lost all the ground he'd gained and then some when his free-spending saddled voters all over Buffalo Ford Township with embarrassing checks they had to redeem with their own money!"

He chuckled and added, "Don't ever endow a nester with the price of a new sunflower windmill and have your check returned after they order said windmill from Chicago if you ever expect that voter to vote you in as dogcatcher! The overconfident fool didn't have the sense to pull in his horns when we *told* him his funds were getting low. He just smiled that sneery way he smiles and told us to let *him* worry about covering all the paper he was hanging. To hear him talk, I was afraid poor little Tess here was up against unlimited funding. Harrison in Cheyenne kept getting fresh funds in the form of unsigned cashier's checks from all over the country."

Tess asked, looking relieved that Longarm hadn't created a scene, how on earth you sent an unsigned check that was any good.

Her portly white-haired swain explained expansively, "You sign the check you pay the bank cashier, who signs *his* name to the iron-bound certified check he sends on for you, backed by his bank's full credit and cashable on delivery."

He smiled at Longarm and added, "None of those have been coming in to cover the handouts of Big Dick Wilcox for some time. I doubt he's still in Wyoming. I know he went busted, to leave irate former friends holding worse than worthless paper all over Laramie County. I understand he wrote worthless checks in the county seat as well. How did you know that was going to happen before the election, Longarm?"

Longarm shrugged and replied, "Stood to reason nobody's pockets could go down forever. Knew he never intended to keep all those promises he was making to clean out the very lowlifes backing his play for the job of Miss Tess here."

Kraft nodded, but said, "You'd have thought he'd pay more attention to simple arithmetic. False promises cost nothing. But when you hand out flashy checks, they snap back and sting you when you don't have money in your account to cover them."

Tess knew Longarm better, and now that she felt more free to talk to him, she asked flat out, "Custis, did you steal that con man's bank deposits?"

Longarm smiled down at her and asked, "How could I or anybody else do that, Miss Tess? Old Herb here or his pal Harrison in Cheyenne would have caught me sure if I'd tried anything that sassy."

Herb Kraft agreed that was true, and they all headed back the way Longarm had just come, seeing it was going on sundown by then and they served warm snacks from a steam table at the Harvest Dance.

They were holding it outdoors on a temporary pine dance floor, it hardly ever raining in Wyoming in the fall. They had Chinese paper lanterns and crepe streamers hung up all around, with the refreshing stand on the downwind side and the bandstand on the upwind side to back

175

the brass, the reeds, and fiddles. The dance hadn't commenced as yet, but the dance floor and grass all around were getting crowded as Longarm parted company with the happy couple to get in line for some hot dogs and root beer. He saw young Deputy Saul Tanner headed his way with Miss Sue Ellen from the library, but before he could howdy them, a voice from the edge of the lantern light snarled, "I knew you'd come back, Longarm!"

So Longarm turned with his hot dog in one hand and root beer in the other to face the white-clad and black-headed but red-faced Big Dick Wilcox, who raved on. "I don't know how you done it, but I know you done it and I don't care how you done it, you son of a bitch!"

So seeing Big Dick seemed so het up as he was going for his Dance Dragoons, Longarm let go of his hot dog and went for his own .44-40 as a gal in the crowd screamed like she'd stubbed her toe.

Then everybody was screaming as Longarm beat Big Dick to the draw and fired first.

The late James Butler Hickok, pontificating to the press as he was getting dangerously famous, had opined it was best to aim between a man's belly button and his groin, since a man hit yonder felt too distracted to fire back whether dead or alive. But Longarm's hot lead lodged in Big Dick's hipbone to spin him around and lay him in the dry grass, squealing like a stuck pig as Longarm moved in fast to kick both holstered six-guns out of their holsters.

As Marshal Brenner joined Longarm over the downed Texan to say he'd seen the son of a bitch slap leather first, Big Dick recovered enough to glare up at Longarm and groan, "Fuck you! Go on and shoot me, now that you've turned every man's hand against me somehow!"

To which Longarm could only reply, not unkindly, "Why should I want to do that, Big Dick? It ain't as if I owe you any favors!"

176

Chapter 20

Everybody there but Big Dick thought Longarm was a good sport not to prefer charges against a man who'd come at him with a brace of Dance Dragoons. Big Dick and Longarm both knew Laredo or somebody as bad would be waiting for him when he got out of the charity ward of Laramie General, and Longarm had enough paperwork to cope with up Wyoming way.

He spent the night after the dance in Buffalo Ford, where old Beth at the Box Elder seemed mighty glad to see him again.

The next day at the inquest in Cheyenne, they didn't take long to decide the scoped Springfield .45–70 Gordo Vance had deposited on the rug of Longarm's hired room after busting into it seemed sufficient evidence for Longarm's plea of self-defense, and Gordo's death was ruled a premeditated suicide.

Longarm caught a southbound night train without looking to see whether old Beverly was on duty in the dining room or not. It sure beat all, he told himself, how unfair human feelings were. For anyone could see that what was good for the goose was sauce for the gander, and yet they said even whores got pissed when they saw a gent they'd

177

diddled eleven gents back go into a crib with another whore. Everybody had the same impossible dream of a world where they got to screw everybody, only nobody else got to screw anybody else.

When he got back to Denver again, and showed up for work feeling stiff from dozing off and on aboard that night train, Henry handed him another perfumed envelope and asked, "Why don't you take pity on the poor lovesick lawyer gal? She's been in here more than once with dumb excuses about working on a federal case down the hall."

Longarm tore open the envelope to see Portia had invited him to supper at her place, Lord willing and the creeks didn't rise, any time he got back from Wyoming.

So the day dragged on forever with him serving a warrant out Aurora way that morning, and pulling courtroom duty down the hall all afternoon, with the willowy brunette Portia Parkhurst, Attorney at Law, never there that day.

Then at last it was quitting time, and since he hadn't informed any other gals he was back in town yet, Longarm was free to pick up some candied ginger and a bouquet of fall mums on his way to Portia's place.

When she came to the door in a house robe to see him standing there, she hauled him inside, kicked the door shut behind him, and tried to suck his tongue out by the roots as she groped at his fly. So he tossed the flowers and candy on a sofa in passing as he carried her on into her bedroom, assuming he was forgiven.

As she let go of him so he could undress, Portia shucked her robe and husked, "Hurry! I feel so awful I misjudged you so, and now I can't wait to make it up to you!"

Longarm said it was swell she felt so forgiving, and not wanting to rock the boat, didn't ask her what she was forgiving him for until they'd torn off the first new leaf and he was trying for another in her dog-style.

Holding her shapely hips to either side of the view he was staring down at with a dirty grin, Longarm observed he hadn't knowingly done anything dirty to her in recent memory.

Her cheek pressed to the rumpled sheets as she thrust back at him with her spine arched to take it deep. Portia purred, "I know. I said I'd misjudged you, silly me. I knew you'd probably do this very thing to my old school chum, Tess Hayward, but what are friends for and I knew she was in serious trouble. I was angry with you because we both thought you'd used and abused her only to desert her in her time of need! The wire she sent me when you lit out on her like that last month was so filled with self-loathing and despair!"

"Did she tell you that last time I came calling on her up yonder she was in bed with her banker?"

Portia laughed and said, "No, but knowing Tess, that dosen't surprise me as much as it must have surprised you. The point is, we both thought you'd just packed it in and left her to fend for herself against overwhelming odds."

Longarm turned Portia over on her back as any man would have at that stage along the primrose path. After they came again, he told her in a calmer tone, "I might have had no choice, had the other side been content to play dirty as usual and not get *personal* with this child. Four years ago our Town-Taming Tess won her position as District Attorney of Buffalo Ford Township fair and square to keep her own promises and clean the township up, to the extent pragmatic and legal. She got the township council to appoint better lawmen and pass more civilized local ordinances. She was able to drive some of the blatant lowlifes clean out of town, and get the others to pull in their horns and behave themselves. It really burned the brimstone out of them."

Portia murmured, "Don't take it out. Let it soak as you

179

explain what you did up there, to her enemies, not to Tess. Could she do *this* for you, dear?"

Longarm laughed and thrust in reply to her playful twitch before he said, "I told you about her banker. I never went to all that work in her behalf because I was driven mad by her flesh. I told Big Dick Wilcox I'd have figured my hands were tied had he been dealing with his money alone. When I saw he was capable of getting his own pals killed, I knew it was my duty as a peace officer to see he never got elected to serve and protect the general public."

"How did you learn who was backing Wilcox with all those campaign contributions, Custis?" she asked.

He said, "I never tried to guess half the names, once I saw the big picture. It didn't matter. There was no mystery as to who was doing what to whom, once I saw Big Dick *doing* it. He even handed me one of his show-off checks, signed with a flourish, the dumb simp. Big Dick was only the tip of the iceberg, a loudmouthed Texas show-off the lowlifes Tess had tamed recruited to buy the election with flashy gestures. They'd chipped in a few dollars each to back his play in the certainty they'd get it all back with interest as soon as they got him elected and he took the lid off a once-more wide-open cow town just outside the city limits of Cheyenne. I'd tell you the sort of entertainment the soiled doves of Red Light Row had planned for right on Main Street if I didn't know you'd suspect me of learning their plans from experience."

She asked how he'd kept the naughty gals and their naughty pimps from taking the town back.

He said, "I figured if Big Dick couldn't hand out any more cheap flash, or better yet, if his cheap flash commenced to be worthless, nobody would vote for him after all. I understand that's the way the voters of Buffalo Ford Township felt when they started to find themselves stuck with stuff they'd ordered and couldn't pay for."

Portia twitched internally again and insisted, "That's

not what I asked you, Custis. I asked you how on earth you *did* it!"

He said, "Let's just say I did it and let it go at that. You and Tess both being officers of the court and all."

She marveled, "I *knew* you'd done something crooked, and aren't you ashamed of yourself, Deputy U.S. Marshal Custis Long?"

"Of the Denver District Court, not Laramie County or the Cheyenne Federal District, and I was off duty on my own time, even if what we did was a federal offense, and I ain't sure it was."

"Let me be the judge of that, speaking as your lawyer." She smiled up at him adoringly.

Longarm said, "Ain't sure you want to know. I *know* Tess Hayward wants to feel she won fair and square when she wins in just a few weeks."

Portia said, "I promise I won't tell. Cross my heart and hope to die, but Jesus, Custis, I'm a fucking *lawyer* fucking you and you have to tell me how you *did* it!"

He said, "Later," as he buried his face in her unbound silver-fox hair to finish what his old organ grinder demanded if she wouldn't let him take it out.

Portia rode to glory with him, her long slender legs locked around his waist as her bare heels rode his heaving buttocks. Then they were snuggled side by side, gasping for their second winds, and being a woman, she repeated her demands.

He said, "Once I figured out their game, like I said, I didn't see any lawful way to stop 'em. There ought to be, but there ain't no laws saying you can't back a hobo off a train passing through for a run at any elective office with your own money, if that's your fancy, and there's no law saying the bum has to disclose where his backing might be coming from if he don't choose to."

"We've been over all that, Custis," she sighed.

He said, "My first thought was to expose Big Dick's

181

backers as the lowlifes they really were. But that meant endless paperwork with no guarantee any prospective voter who'd just had his mortgage paid off or a new well bored on his pig farm would *care* who Big Dick's *other* friends might be. You're sure this is a priviliged converstation betwixt a country boy who means well and the attorney he's in bed with?"

Portia said, "You pulled the rug out from under him and left him hanging worthless paper all over the electoral district he was out to win! So how in blue blazes did you *do* it, damn it?"

Longarm said, "He gave me the notion himself when he handed me a generous-looking check I couldn't cash because it was made out to my undertaker. I got to studying on how many of his show-off checks were worth the paper they were written on. Then I got to studying on how others might feel if they found themselves staring at a show-off check they couldn't cash. Then I tried to recall ever reading any statute book saying what I had in mind was against the law, and when I saw nobody had ever passed any laws covering events unlikely to happen, I carried the four-flusher's worthless check, bearing his *signature*, to a convicted forger I knew up that way."

"You, a sworn peace officer, working with a wanted outlaw?" she gasped.

Longarm said, "Aw, he ain't wanted. He was convicted, like I said, and served his time. His wife and me had this same discussion as I was recruiting them to help me. I told her, as I hope you'll assure me, forgery is only a felony when you forge someone's signature to steal money. It's just a sort of . . . *prank* when you ain't making a dime out of it, right?"

Portia said, "Custis, that's pure sophistry and you know it. It's not *nice* to forge another person's signature or handwriting. But go ahead. What did you naughty boys sign Big Dick Wilcox in his very own hand?"

Longarm answered simply, "Checks. He wasn't all that nice neither, and seeing he seemed so anxious to be known as a Lord Bountiful writing checks for worthy causes, we let him contribute to some worthy causes."

"You didn't!" She laughed wildly as she got the picture.

Longarm said, "Sure we did. It was easy, and once we got started, fun. We had his worried wife laughing fit to bust when she addressed a handsome donation to Miss Victoria Woodhull's feminist party so's she can run for President this fall, and not wanting to leave other ladies out, we naturally sent a handsome donation to the Women's Christian Temperance Union. Then there was, let's see, the Republican Party, the Democratic Party, the National Grange, and of course old Single Tax George. Big Dick wanted it known he was a swell gent who liked everybody, and we just helped him sell the grand notion by letting him send a healthy contribution to every worthy cause I had blank checks for. But we never diverted a dime of his campaign money for *ourselves,* and as a matter of fact, I was out the postage!"

Portia wriggled sideways into a more relaxed position as she told him, "Speaking as your lawyer, now that we've come, no matter how you slice it, you just plain broke the law, Custis."

Longarm wriggled them both closer to the head of her bed atop her pillows as he replied, "So's buying a responsible Indian a drink. So's what we've been doing, and at this moment, all over the land, men and women we'd call honest are committing crimes against nature that more than one state would give them twenty years in prison for. Speaking as a man empowered to enforce laws sensible or not, there's the fine print of the law and then there's the higher law of common decency. Big Dick was fixing to steal that election, fair and square under statute law. There wasn't an honest move our side could have made if we couldn't match his resources dollar for dollar. So I crooked a crook, and if that be treason, make the most of it."

Portia laughed and said, "Forgery is felony, not treason, Patrick Henry!"

Longarm replied defensively, "Well, wasn't *he* committing a hanging offense in a higher cause?"

She said, "You don't have to convince *me*! I was a good friend of Tess Hayward before I sent you up there to just plain break the law for her higher cause. But you never should have let Big Dick Wilcox live when he gave you such a good excuse to kill him, Custis!"

He snuggled her closer, kissed the part in her silver-flecked black hair, and explained, "I *had* to shoot to stop him without killing him. Shooting a man in self-defense is one thing. Shooting a man to shut him up is murder. Us felons in a higher cause have to draw the line somewheres."

She reached down between them to fondle him as he went on. "I never wanted a gunfight with him. I was hoping he'd pack it in and crawl off to wherever he came from when his own pals and former admirers turned on him. To this very night he dosen't know how I pulled the rug out from under him, but he figured out who'd done it. I made the mistake of telling him he'd riled me before I showed a dirty dealer how to get down and dirty."

As Portia began to slowly and thoughtfully stroke him, she decided, "Speaking as the defense counsel you'll need if he ever finds out what you and that convicted forger did to his war chest, we *may* get you off with minimum time on the grounds you were diverting ill-gotten gains to worthy causes for no personal profit. But I still say you should have shot him when you had the excuse!"

Longarm said he doubted Big Dick was capable of suspecting anybody would do anything truly generous for anybody else. Then Longarm rolled back in the saddle, and he wasn't really worried, or didn't feel really worried as he got to work a few mornings later after breakfast in another bed.

As he came in, Henry asked if he'd seen the early edition of the *Rocky Mountain News*. When Longarm confided he'd only been served ham and eggs with his wake-up coffee, Henry said, "That political slicker you had that trouble with up Wyoming way made the front page."

Longarm wondered how come his mouth was suddenly so dry as he asked in a desperately casual tone, "Big Dick Wilcox? How did he make the front page, Henry?"

The clerk typist said, "They shot him dead in his hospital bed up at Laramie General. A deputy sheriff visiting with his wife down the hall got the ones who did it. Hired guns called Laredo Nolan and a younger cuss called Truman. When the Wyoming lawman saw 'em coming out of the charity ward with smoking six-guns in their hands . . . what did I just say to make you look so queer? You look like a fool kid coming in his pants!"

To which Longarm could only reply, "That's about the size of it, and ain't it a wonder how worried a man can be without half noticing it up to the moment he sees he has nothing to worry about after all?"

Watch for

Longarm and the Kissin' Cousins

298th novel in the exciting LONGARM series
from Jove

Coming in September!

Explore the exciting Old West with one of the men who made it wild!